The Shifting Sea

Lauren Sanatra

**Copyright © 2020 by Lauren Sanatra.
All rights reserved.**

No part of this publication may be reproduced. Stored in a retrieval system, or transmitted in any form or by any means, electronic, mechanical, photocopying, recording, or otherwise, without written permission of the author.

This is a work of fiction. Names, characters, places, and incidents either are the product of the author's imagination or are used fictitiously. Any resemblance to actual persons, live or dead are purely coincidental.

Original title:
Whispers of the Snowman's Smile

Copyright © 2024 Creative Arts Management OÜ
All rights reserved.

Author: Lila Davenport
ISBN HARDBACK: 978-9916-94-390-8
ISBN PAPERBACK: 978-9916-94-391-5

Icebound Revelry

On a winter's day so bright,
The snowman danced, oh what a sight!
With carrot nose and buttons round,
He wobbled and laughed without a sound.

The kids would join with gleeful cheer,
Tossing snowballs, never fear!
He'd trip and tumble, oh such grace,
Leaving snow prints all over the place.

The Echo of Frosted Joy

In a field of glistening white,
Stood a snowman basking in the light.
He chuckled at a passing pet,
With snowflakes sticking like a vignette.

His button eyes sparkled and shone,
As he told jokes in a frosty tone.
The squirrels paused, their cheeks so round,
As laughter bubbled from the ground.

Snow's Cheery Companion

By the hill where children play,
A jolly figure brightens the day.
With arms outstretched, he greets his fans,
Dictating rules to snowy plans.

He spins and twirls on frosty toes,
A ballet among the flakes that blows.
With every slip and sliding slide,
He waves his hat, full of winter pride.

Frost's Animated Grin

With snowflakes bouncing off his head,
That merry snowman shimmered red.
With a toothy grin, he stole the scene,
As kids made snowballs and formed a team.

The wind picked up, the snowflakes flew,
He juggled them as children cooed.
Falling flat with laughter shared,
His silly antics clearly aired.

Giggles in the Cold

In winter's grip, the snowflakes dance,
Chilly cheeks in a frosty trance.
Snowmen grin with buttons bright,
Tickling snowballs, a playful sight.

Laughter echoes through the trees,
As snowflakes melt on noses with ease.
A snowman winks, his scarf askew,
While kids in mittens throw snowballs too!

Hot cocoa waits by the fire's glow,
But first, we'll play in the white below.
Winter's joy is loud and clear,
Giggles ringing from ear to ear.

Secrets of the Chilly Veil

Behind the snow, a secret hides,
In drifts so deep, where fun abides.
Snowmen chuckle and nod in glee,
Whispering jokes as cold as can be.

With carrot noses, they plot and scheme,
To tease the children with playful dreams.
Snowballs launch with a whoosh and cheer,
As winter giggles, it's plain to hear.

Hats may be crooked, a scarf on the floor,
But the laughter outside will always score!
Frosty friends share a wink and a jig,
In the snowy chaos, they dance big.

The Smirking Snowman

A snowman stands with a cheeky grin,
Ready to cause a giggle or spin.
His eyes of coal, so shiny and bright,
Sparkle with mischief on a snowy night.

With a twist and a turn, he's up to no good,
Launching snowballs like he said he would.
Laughter erupts as they scatter and fly,
While kids around him gasp and sigh.

A raucous game, as snowflakes twirl,
Creating smiles in a frosty whirl.
A smirking snowman, the king of play,
Brings giggles and joy to the snowy ballet.

Table of Contents

Chapter 1 1

Chapter 2 14

Chapter 3 24

Chapter 4 39

Chapter 5 57

Chapter 6 86

Chapter 7 107

Epilogue 125

Frosted Whimsy

In the hush of snow, where laughter leans,
Frosted whimsy flows in playful scenes.
Chubby snowmen with ribbons bright,
Join in the fun, hearts feel light.

Snowflakes tumble, all shapes and size,
Gathering giggles under the skies.
A snowball fight, oh what a scene,
With frosty friends—what a festive routine!

Do they tell tales of snowy delight?
In the chilly air, their laughter ignites.
Frosty figures with joy on display,
Spread the cheer in a fun-filled array.

Frosty Secrets Revealed

In the cold where snowflakes fall,
A frosty friend stands proud and tall.
Carrot nose and button eyes,
He's plotting fun beneath winter skies.

With a wink, he gives a cheer,
Telling tales for all to hear.
He rolls and tumbles, giggles abound,
In the chill, his laughter's found.

Snowballs fly with silly grace,
Dodging frost, a merry chase.
A curly scarf wraps 'round his neck,
This playful chap, what the heck!

Under moonlight, secrets shared,
Frosty jokes, he really dared.
His snowy form, a jester's guise,
In every flake, a giggle lies.

The Grin Beneath the Snow

Beneath the layers, smiles awake,
   Frosty fun with every flake.
He hides his jokes in drifts so deep,
   With chuckles, he can hardly keep.

His coal eyes twinkle, full of glee,
   A winter prankster, wild and free.
Sleds and snowmen, playful vie,
   Catching laughter as it flies.

When kids come by to build him right,
He throws a snowball for pure delight.
   Frosty tricks to make hearts race,
   In every scoop, a funny face.

At dusk he twirls, with arms out wide,
   In snow-laden joy, he takes a ride.
The grin upon his frosty skin,
Turns winter's chill to giggles within.

Silent Joy of Winter

In silence soft, the snowflakes play,
Transforming town in bright array.
A jolly heart beneath the frost,
Lives laughter small, not at a loss.

With a jig, he hops along,
To the rhythm of winter's song.
Pants of snow and hat so grand,
Creating joy with a frosty hand.

As kids come running, squeals of glee,
His frozen heart skips merrily.
A warm embrace beneath the cold,
With tales of fun forever told.

In quiet nights, a snowman dreams,
Of snowy capers and silly schemes.
With each new flake, a spark ignites,
Through winter's hush, he shares delights.

Chapter 1

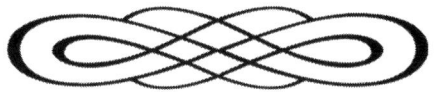

Daniel stood at the stern of the ship as he watched the dark waves turn white with foam as the ship continued underway. Breathing in the salty sea air as the ship continued out, the port became smaller and smaller. Eventually, with no land in sight, it was clear that the crew and himself must be somewhere in the middle of the Atlantic Ocean. Deep in thought about the new venture his father, Captain Charles the Dread, had now assigned to the crew, Daniel could not help but have a worried expression permanently frozen to his face.

"Daniel!" a rough voice shouted from behind, breaking Daniel from his trance.

"Yes Father?" Daniel asked as he turned around, coming face to face with his father.

"What is it you are doin' back here boy?" Captain Charles asked with a look and tone of annoyance in his voice.

"I am sorry father, I was-"

"No excuses, now get upfront," Charles scolded as he pushed Daniel towards the bow of the ship. "You want to set a good example for your future crew now eh?"

Daniel reluctantly nodded as he and Captain Charles marched to the front of the ship. Not only had Daniel inherited his father's coal black hair with a set of cerulean blue eyes, but he would soon inherit his father's crew and his ship "The Grey Siren". Being born into the life of piracy really left a man with nothing but dishonor and judgement from those back on land. This was a life Daniel had never wanted. But in the year 1723 and being the son of a pirate with such a reputation as his father's, there were not many options in his favor. While Daniel inherited his father's looks and soon his ship, he inherited the most important thing from his late mother, compassion. Daniel promised himself he would never let "Dread" be attached to his title when he was captain.

Daniel gathered what remained of the crew to the front of the ship, to go over the plan yet again. Captain Charles the Dread had rightfully earned his name, causing the crew to grow smaller and smaller with each season.

Some would leave on their own accord and for their own safety, while others could not escape Charles's impeachable temper and wrath, often resulting in their unmarked watery graves. The crew now only consisted of nine other men besides Daniel and his father. Despite Captain Charles the Dread living up to his reputation of being the scourge of the seven seas, he was also the most successful when it came to locating, plundering and coveting the most booty. This was enough incentive for men to stay aboard and endure his cruelty.

Of the nine men, only two were veteran seadogs. The other seven were new to the ship, being on board only a few weeks now, and some only a few days. Felix and August had been a part of the crew for the last eleven years, ever since Daniel was a boy of only nine years old. Though their years of work and hardships were evident on their chapped and wrinkled faces, they were a loyal duo.

As the men were assembled, Daniel tucked his baggy stained white blouse into his breeches, adjusted his black leather vest and took his place next to his father as first mate. As Daniel stared at the faces of the men he knew would be doomed after this particular quest, he started to take into account that he himself may not survive this one. It was basically a suicide mission that no man, nor woman, had ever lived to tell the tale about.

Captain Charles took a step forward, addressing the crew, "Now, we all know the plan, but for some of you new buccs, me thinks its best that we go over it one more time, aye?" Charles announced as he flourished his arm up towards the sky to rally the men.

"Aye!" yelled the crew almost in perfect unison.

"Men, we are to take the daring journey to the Isles of the Blessed where we shall find and capture the legendary silver sea serpent!" Charles shouted which was met with an echo of cheers from the crew. "When we find the beast, we shall follow the markings upon its back to the fabled treasure of wonders!"

Once again, the men cheered, all but one, a young man about Daniel's age, maybe even a bit younger, who was new to the crew. The young man stepped forward to present his question and concern. "But sir, no one has ever come back from such a journey, and no one is daft enough to try to find the monster."

The young lad stood there looking up at his captain with his wide innocent eyes, hoping for an answer. In that quick moment, Daniel could see his father's face grow red and clenched as he began reaching for his pistol, ready to set an example of the new crew member. Daniel swiftly spoke up to deescalate what could have been the end of this young man's short life.

"Let me handle this one" Daniel quickly chimed in, gently putting his hand on his father's arm to retract the pistol. "Well sir," Daniel began as he cleared his throat to project his voice with false confidence, "to rebuttal your statement, no one has gone against The Grey Siren and Captain Charles the Dread and lived to tell the tale, I expect no differently when we find this sea serpent." Daniel finished as he took a step back in his place beside his father.

"Plus," August, an old salt, chimed in "the said treasure, that the markings on the beast will lead us to, are fabled to be worth more than the King England himself. This is a no prey, no pay job!"

A smile shone across the young crew member's face as the words from Daniel and August were enough to satisfy his doubt and to feed his greed. He quickly took his place back with the crew as they all began to tend to their individual jobs and post.

The ship continued at an incredible speed as they made way towards their goal destination. The Grey Siren was not the biggest compared to other ships, however in this case, it was not the size that counted, rather what the crew at the commands of Captain Charles did with it. A smaller ship meant a smaller crew which meant less people to share the booty with. Small and horrifying was the ships reputation. Most privateers and fellow pirates feared this ship, even ships with twice as many crew members knew to avoid the ghostly grey sails if they should come in its path. Fear was how Captain Charles ruled, something Daniel never agreed with.

The day began to shift into night, trading the sun and clouds for the moon and stars, as the ship continued to sail with ease toward the Isle of the Blessed. At the rate they were traveling, they could easily reach their destination before the sunset the next day. The only problem was, would they find the sea serpent just as easily. Little was known about the creature, leaving only stories and myths to go off of. For years a piece of parchment was passed around from town to town with a rendering of the markings that would surely be on the serpents back. These renderings, however, were only ever used as examples. It was the writing on the parchment of the serpent's whereabouts that was important if any man were to attempt to locate the treasure. Even though many had gone missing after their endeavors, the fabled reward was enough to entice many to make the journey to capture the beast and track the treasure for themselves.

Watching his father steer through the night, Daniel finally had the courage to say what he had been thinking since the beginning of this quest. "Father," Daniel said in a low and calm voice, "You know, if we survive this, and if the treasure is as grand as you say, why not retire, the both of us, hell the entire crew and leave this life behind us?"

An uncomfortable silence filled the air as Charles stared at Daniels innocent face. "Retire?" he sternly replied. "Danny boy, piracy is in our blood and enough treasure is never enough! Are you not proud to be taking my place as Captain?"

"No, it's not that, it's just," Daniel paused to come up with the right words as not to anger his father. "We may not even survive this, not all of us at least, and if we do, why can't we leave it at that and enjoy our spoils? You are getting older, and it is getting harder and harder to get men to join your insane ventures-"

"Insane ventures? This is the kind of talk and doubt a captain does not want to hear from his first mate, let alone his own flesh and blood," Charles replied as he removed his hands from the wheel to face his son. "I am the Captain and I make the calls, once I leave you the ship and crew you can make those decisions, but til' then I am in charge!" he said coldly through his clenched teeth.

Daniel knew there was no reasoning with his father. He knew talk like that from anyone else in the crew, it would have been there end or at the very least a keelhaul, but since he was his son, Daniel had always hoped Charles would listen to reason and logic from him. Yet again, he was unsuccessful. The sea and piracy was always his father's only love, *maybe even more then him and his own mother*, Daniel thought. That was his final push to get Charles to change his ways and have a new mindset. Deep down he knew he would never agree, but he had to try.

The sea air grew colder and colder as the ship continued to sail through the night. The crew decided to take dinner in shifts to make sure the ship was moving steadily along to their destination. Daniel, Charles, Felix and August went below deck for the first dining shift. Dinner was never anything too fancy for the rest of the scallywags, but for these four, it was always the best of what there was to offer. Beef roast, various cheeses, fresh grapes, olives and of course some spiced wine and rum to wash it all down. Being close to the captain and in his good graces came with the perk of fine food while the rest of the crew would have meatless stew, some stale bread, and if they were lucky, a few sips of wine and rum that was not finished and turned into grog.

As the four pirates indulged in their meal and imbibed with their wine and rum, the tension that was feeding into the air from Daniel and Charles started to fade. More drinks led to a more relaxed Charles. Seeing the opportunity of Charles's good spirits, Felix and August decided it was safe enough to talk about his plan in capturing the sea serpent.

"So," Felix started as he took a gulp from his chalice, "according to legend, this thing is spose' to be twenty feet long, after we catch it, where is it you plan on stashing the beast?"

"I have one of the young lads knocking down the cell bars down below to make one long cage for the beast." Charles replied as he sat back bloated and full from his meal.

"And killin' the thing is out of the question right?" August asked as he was picking food from the few teeth he had left in his mouth. "Might just be easier, not to mention safer for us all."

"I told you before, if we kill it and can't decipher the map on the beast's back in time, the dead corpse may start to shrivel and rot, rendering the map unreadable, not to mention the smell." Charles calmly said as he took a swig of rum from the bottle and chased it with some wine from his chalice.

"Do you think the new boys will live?" Felix asked with a hint of compassion in his voice.

"If they don't," Charles started holding back a small laugh, "more treasure for us."

After being silent throughout dinner, Daniel finally spoke out towards his father's last comment. "So is that all they are, dispensable to you? You know that one young man who spoke out earlier can't be any older then I am, maybe even a year or so younger!" Daniel snapped as he slammed his glass against the table causing the stim of his chalice to shatter.

"Uh, Daniel maybe you shouldn't..." August started as he moved his arm towards Daniel to hold him back.

"Again with this!" Charles shouted, removing him from his prior relaxed state. "This is the way we have always done it, you know that! These men knew what they were getting into so I apologize if I have no sympathy of these boys' lives potentially being lost in pursuit of their own greed!" Charles yelled as he started to put on his coat, preparing to head above deck. "Now, I don't want to hear another word about it. You will do your job, the crew will do theirs and if a little blood is spilled, then so be it!" With that, Charles marched up the steps towards the deck.

The three men finished there drinks in silence, scared to comment on Captain Charles recent outburst. Finally, after a few moments of the awkward silence, Felix reached out towards Daniel and gave him a gentle squeeze on the shoulder, "Look, I've known you since you were a mere lad, why are ye now fighting your obligation and duty to your Captain?"

"Every city we have pillaged and burned to the ground, every ship we have captured, people we have enslaved, all for something shiny to fill our greedy hearts," Daniel started as his eyes filled with tears, "I just can't do this anymore, and the sea serpent? No one has survived and I am not ready to die for treasure, no matter how grand. Are you?"

"Well," August chimed in, "I think I speak for Felix and myself when I say aye. Danny boy we are old and this is the life we chose to live. Your father has been talking about this quest for the fabled treasure for years, and now with time no longer on our side, what do we have to lose?"

"Those men up there, those young men too blinded by the glitter my father sold them in his tale, they don't deserve this." Daniel softly replied as his eyes traced towards the wooden ceiling.

Felix gave Daniel's arm another gentle squeeze, "You too Danny, your life is important too, but between you and your father, I am sure we can pull it off. Don't forget, we've seen you grow through the years, not only into a good man, but a pretty decent swordsman and fighter." Felix finished as he gave Daniel a small smile. "You will make a great captain."

With their dinner shift done, August gathered the other crew members to enjoy their meal, well what there was of it anyways, as Daniel took his place by his father as they sailed through the night.

As the sun began to rise, their surroundings became lit and more visible. They were on the right path. They knew they would reach the Isle of the Blessed before the sun departed the sky for the night. It was time to prepare for the attack on the sea serpent that would take place in just a few hours.

Chapter 2

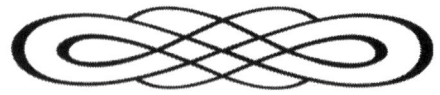

The Grey Siren continued steady on its course as the crew began to prepare the canons. The plan was to blast it with the smaller cannonballs, since the goal was to capture it alive. Wounding it was fine, but killing it was not part of Charles's plan. After the canons were loaded, the men brought a large net that was fashioned from at least twenty single ones to from one large final net, up to the ship deck. After wounding the serpent, the plan was to drag the beast from the water in the makeshift net, throw it in the cell, and hopefully in its weak state, they would be able to safely read the map upon its back. Daniel would stand by, sword in hand just in case the plan needed to be altered. Everything was ready, but now, their greatest mission, maybe even more difficult than capturing it, was where to find it.

All they knew were small details that had been passed down from story to story and pirate to pirate from the piece of faded parchment, of where the sea serpent had been spotted and have heard stories. Now it was time to see if the stories were true. It had been told that the minute a ship pulls in, it sets the serpent into a frenzy, ready to take down the ship and all that inhabit it. As dangerous as this sounded, this is what Captain Charles was banking on. The sooner the serpent showed itself, the sooner they could capture it, translate the map, and be on their way to treasures untold.

They sailed closer and closer and could even make out an image in the distance. Daniel and Charles squinted their tired eyes to make out the image.

Taking out a small spyglass from his satchel, Daniel raised it to his eye to observe the image, "It's another ship." Daniel flatly stated.

"A what!" Charles shouted causing the whole crew to be startled. "So they think they can find the beast before we do huh?" he stated before raising his sword, "Felix, fire a cannon their way!"

Daniel quickly turned to his father, "Wait, we don't have to do this, we don't even know if that's why they are here, they could just be lost. Why not run a shot across the bow?" Daniel pleaded. "Besides, once they see the grey sails, they will surely turn back." Daniel finished as tried to stop his father's orders.

"Fire!" Charles shouted over his sons pleas'.

Felix lit the fuse, sending a cannonball straight for the ship. Snatching the spyglass from Daniel's hand, Charles stared out at his successful attack as the ship was hit. They waited a few moments before wasting another cannon ball on the ship ahead.

"What's going on Captain? Should I fire another?" Felix shouted from below.

"Not necessary, seems they have spotted our sails, they are turning back."

A sigh of relief swept over Daniel as he assisted his father in steering the ship forward. *Hopefully the ship ahead stays out of the way,* Daniel thought to himself. The last thing he wanted was more lives lost.

A thick fog rolled in as they approached their final destination. This was it. They had safely made it to the Isle of the Blessed. Show time.

"Throw the anchor!" Charles shouted to one of newer crew members. "Now we wait."

An hour had passed, still no sign of the sea serpent. The crew, though growing impatient, remained in their positions, ready to fire on the captain's command. Two hours had passed, still nothing.

"Maybe it's just what it was, a story, it never existed." Daniel softly said to his father.

"No," Charles replied, his eyes still fixated on the water, "It can't be just a tale, it just can't be. I have known pirates who ne're returned from this voyage. It's here I know it. We must be patient."

The sun had set, and still there was silence from the dark waters. A thick blanket of fog almost completely covered the ocean below, making it harder and harder to inspect.

"Captain, sir," August shouted from below, "Some of us are having trouble keeping our eyes open down here and it doesn't look like this creature is showing up anytime soon, should we start some sleep shifts and have them men take a caulk?'

"No! It will show, just you wait." Charles yelled back.

Though he was tired, Daniel couldn't help but feel at ease that he may be right and that the legends of the sea serpent were just stories. No one had to fight, no one had to die, they could say they tried and could move on from there. Just as a small smile started to form on Daniel's face, it was instantly transformed to worry as something below shook the entire ship.

"This is it lads!" Charles shouted with glee in his voice. "Get ready, all hands on deck!"

Though the fog was thick, apparent movement was in the water. This was their chance. The crew took their place awaiting the captain's orders. The ship continuously rocked as the serpent below tried to drag it down.

"It's under us captain!" August yelled, clinging to his cannon for stability. "We need to move the ship!"

"We can't lose it! We stay where we are," Charles shouted back as he himself hung to his wheel to stay grounded.

"Father, it will capsize us, we have to do something!" Daniel pleaded with his father.

"It just needs a distraction," Charles replied as he started to head down to the crew, hanging on to the bannister as the ship continued to rock.

"What are you doing?" Daniel asked as he watched his father head towards the young crew member who had questioned him earlier. "What are you doing?"

Captain Charles promptly grabbed the young man from his cannon and dragged him to the starboard side.

"Stop, please, captain stop!" the young man pleaded as he waved his arms wildly about, trying to free himself from Charles' grip.

"It's for the greater good,' Charles responded as he swiftly picked up the young crew member. "Hungry beasty? Here you go!' Charles finished as he tossed the young man overboard.

"No!" Daniel screamed as he rushed towards his father. "You can't do this!"

"Get back to your positon Danny, now!" Charles snapped back.

Daniel looked over the side of the ship at the young lad flapping about in the water to keep his head above the water. The crew had no choice but to ignore the young man's screams and pleas for help, captain's orders.

The ship stopped rocking, and through the thick layer of fog, a shape became visible charging straight for the young crew member bobbing in the water. "There it is! Fire!" Charles shouted as he took his place in front.

The air echoed with the sound of cannon fire as they aimed all forces towards the serpent. Although the creature was still hidden in the fog, they could see it was retreating from the ripples and waves in the water.

"Again!" Charles commanded. Luckily, the serpent was unable to reach the young crew member still struggling in the water. Daniel saw a quick opportunity to save him while his father was solely focused on the movements of the serpent. Daniel ran to the side to lower a rope to aid the young man.

"Grab a hold and I will pull you up!" Daniel shouted down to the half-drowned lad.

The young man did as he was ordered and grabbed the rope tightly as Daniel started to pull him to safety.

Dangling from the rope, the young crew member must have looked like a worm on a hook due to the serpent, now visible and emerging from the water, heading straight toward him. Daniel had to move fast. "It's on the starboard side father! Shoot now!" Daniel yelled, realizing this was the only way to save the man, blast the beast.

More blasts echoed in the air as Daniel was able to pull the man back on board. Still, the serpent was persistent and would not give up. It continued to leap towards the ship's deck, its silver scales glistening in the moonlight. One final leap, and the serpent balanced on the ships bannister, ready to charge at Daniel. Out of instinct, Daniel unsheathed his sword and stabbed the creature before it could make its way fully on the deck.

"Danny's got him!" August hollered.

Silver blood stained his sword as he came face to face with the legendary sea serpent, still skewered on his sword. Looking the serpent in its sapphire blue eyes, and its new docile state, he couldn't help but feel a twinge of compassion. As his eyes remained locked on the serpent's face. He could see nothing but pain in its dilated pupils.

Feeling unthreatened from the injured creature impaled by his sword, he pulled his blade back, letting the beast go.

"No!" Charles screamed as he saw the serpent slither back into the water. "You had him!"

"No," Daniel lied. "It was about to launch at me, I had to retreat."

Visually upset with a red face, Charles barked orders at the crew to remain in position as he stormed to the bow of the ship. His eyes once again glued to the waves below, looking for a twinge of silver beneath the fog.

"Thank you," the young crew member said to Daniel, still catching his breath from his escapades in the water. His teeth chattering from the cold.

"I apologize on behalf of my father, he can be cruel." Daniel replied as he helped the man up on his feet. "What is your name?"

"Peter," the young man said with a cough, "my name is Peter."

"Well, Peter, I hope you realize the price of greed and piracy. You were lucky this time, but don't have the illusion that there will be someone there to save you next time. Pirates don't do that."

"But sir, you did," Peter said with a confused look of innocence on his face.

"I'm not a pirate,' Daniel coldly replied, leaving Peter to think about his choices while he took his place by his father.

Chapter 3

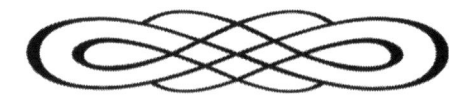

Time had passed, but the serpent had not returned. Daniel scanned the water, but could only see debris floating about from the damage the serpent had brought upon the ship. "Maybe we killed it?" Daniel said as he watched his father obsessively pacing his eyes back and forth toward the water. "Maybe we hit it too hard with the cannon fire, for all we know it has sunk to the bottom of the Atlantic."

"No," Charles said, his eyes still fixated on the water, "This thing can withstand a lot of pain and damage. Plus, like most sea creatures, it would float, have you seen a serpent corpse anywhere Danny boy?"

"No."

"Then we wait. It will come back, trust me."

Knowing there was nothing he could say to make his father turn back and head to port, or any port for that matter, Daniel could only offer a suggestion. "Why don't we move the ship to the other side, maybe it's resting on the other side of the Isle." Anything to get the ship and crew up and running again from their stagnation and uncertainty.

"Now *that's* captain talk," Charles said in approval as he provided Daniel with a playful punch to the shoulder. "You may be right. The beast might be wounded and hiding on the other side trying to recharge, and if it is, we will have a real chance at capturing it."

Charles spat the orders out to the crew and they prepared to sail. The anchor was lifted and the men assumed their positions to go underway. With the sky growing darker and darker as the night loomed on, they would have to be extra stealthy. Sail slowly and cautiously.

The ship trudged along, but there was still no movement in sight. The calm waters began to fill with fog yet again as the hours went by and the night turned cold. All they could do was circle the area, make sure that they covered every inch. After all of this, there was still, nothing from below.

As the ship aimlessly drifted on the water, it was clear to the whole crew, they had missed their chance. There was no way the serpent would return, assuming it was alive that is. They had hit it with all they had. Either it wasn't enough or it was too much. They had come this far, but now it was time to cut their losses, something the crew was fine with after seeing the power of the serpent. However, the Captain was noticeably irritable at their failure.

"We tried Father, but the beast bested us, and we are all alive to tell the tale. There is no shame in losing this one," Daniel softly said to Charles, trying to put him at ease.

Holding back his anger Charles replied, "I know son." He took a deep, cleansing breath, "I was supposed to be the captain that went down in history. I was supposed to be the one to capture the sea serpent and find the fabled treasure. This was going to be my legacy!" he finished, his breaths sharp and mouth clenched.

Scared to say anything further, Daniel stood in silence. His father had lost this one, something he is not used to. He figured he would let him stew in his anger just a bit longer. The last thing Daniel wanted was for his father to take it out on the crew. *Let him fume, and then turn the ship around and head to make port somewhere,* Daniel thought. This was the plan, at least it was until a loud voice from the deck called out.

"Captain!" one of the crew-men called out as he had one eye glued to a spyglass from the crow's nest, "I see something in the water. I can't make it out from here, but it's just there up ahead." The man pointed toward the sea.

Immediately, Daniel and Charles pulled out their own scopes to take a look. They could both see something floating, but, just like the man below, they could not make out what it was in the darkness. Best case scenario, it was the sea serpent's body floating. Worst case, it was the corpse of a shark. Either way, Charles ordered the crew to sail in its direction.

They slowed the ship down as they got closer to better observe whatever it was floating nearby. The whole crew was giddy, hoping they had found the body of the serpent that would lead them to their ultimate payday without having to fight again. Finally close enough, they lowered the anchor. Looking long and hard at the shape in the water below, they were able to make out what it was.

It, unfortunately, was not the sea serpent, now was it the corpse of a shark. It was a human. Its long silver hair covered most of its body clinging to its skin, revealing a small silhouette. It was evident that this was a young woman. She was unconscious, maybe even dead, clinging to a piece of wooden debris to stay afloat. With small patches of red staining her silver hair and pale skin, it was clear if she was not dead already, she would be soon.

"What is it Captain?" Felix called from below.

Looking hard, his brows furrowed, Charles responded, "It's a person, dead from the looks of it."

"It looks like a woman," Daniel added as his eyes stayed fixated on the lifeless body below in the water.

"Damn, well boys, looks like it's not the serpent, let us turn her around and head back to port." Charles ordered as he prepared to take his place to start the journey back. "Weigh the anchor and hoist the mizzen!"

"Wait!" Daniel quickly replied, "We have to help her, she may still be alive!"

"Well then she can swim herself back to shore when she comes to," Charles said as he carried on in getting the ship turned back around, "Let's go boys, bring a spring upon 'er."

The ship started at a quick pace as it started to head back towards the direction they came. Daniel couldn't help but stare back at the poor woman, still motionless in the water. He had to try again.

"Father, she looks hurt. Even if she wakes up, there is no way she can swim anywhere in her condition!" Daniel pleaded.

"Enough!" Charles shouted, "I am not jumping into the icy water to retrieve a corpse and if she were to be alive, we are not adding another mouth to feed on this ship!"

Desperate to find a solution, Daniel did the only thing he could think of at that moment. Standing tall, Daniel proudly exclaimed, "I'll do it then!" as he leaped off the side of the ship into the frigid water below, swimming in pursuit to save the woman.

"Daniel!" Charles screamed as he watched his son plunge into the water. "Damn it," he said under his breath, "stop! turn the ship around!"

"Do you see it Captain? Has the serpent returned?" Felix asked from the deck below

"No, my sorry excuse for a son went overboard. Let's go lads, turn her around!"

With the ship making its way to reclaim Daniel, he knew he had to swim faster. The water was freezing, making every stroke harder and harder. Daniel's breath grew shallower as he beat himself against the waves that lingered from the ship's retreat. He tried to swim as fast as he could while keeping his head above the water, as not to choke on the salty sea below, but it was only slowing him down. He knew the quickest way was to completely submerge himself under using the water to aid each stroke. He had to reach her before the ship got to him. *He had to save to get to her and get there fast,* he thought as he dunked his head under the water to accelerate towards his goal.

Coming up only for quick breathes and to make sure his target was still in sight, he was out swimming the ship, but not by much. He had almost reached her when he heard the echoes of his father's voice above as the ship began to gain on him. Ignoring his calls, Daniel finally reached the woman, still floating on the piece of wood that looked like it was due to capsize any moment.

Brushing her hair from her face, he inspected her. She was breathtakingly beautiful. Pale and soft, but cold skin. Her face resembled those of angels Daniel would see in the many pieces of art he and his father had plundered through the years. On top of her beauty, he could also see wounds throughout her bare body, wounds that would need to be dressed sooner rather than later. Daniel pressed his ear to her chest, being respectful not to infringe on her naked state. He could hear a faint heartbeat that was struggling.

"Miss?" he gently whispered as he held her in his arms while trying to balance them both on the wooden debris. "Miss, can you hear me?"

With no response and the ship literally about to crash into the two, he did the only thing he could remember when someone had taken in too much water. He placed his mouth over hers, hoping to breathe life into her. He repeated this over and over, as he let the sounds of his father yelling from above fade away, focusing only on saving this young woman's life.

A ladder was thrown below to lift Daniel back up. All of which Daniel ignored as he focused on the young woman in his arms. Still simultaneously keeping them both afloat and trying to resuscitate her, though it was coming more difficult, as the debris keeping them up was becoming useless as it began to sink.

"Daniel, just grab the damn ladder!" Charles called from above.

Once again shutting out the rattles from the ship, he finally heard a sound that was music to his ears, a gasp. The woman was breathing, not very well, but she was breathing. That's all that mattered at that moment. She was still in a weak and drowsy state, but she was alive. He had done it; he had saved her.

"Father," Daniel called up, "I'll take the ladder, but only if you pull us both up." Daniel demanded.

Tired of having to argue, he agreed. The crew hoisted Daniel and the woman up and brought them safely to the deck. The men could not help but stare at the woman's naked body. They were thieves and rogues after-all, and it had been some time since a few had been with a woman.

Daniel observed the animalistic stares from the men around him. Daniel himself even snuck an accidental glance at her naked body, but he would never do what he knew some of these men could or have done before to a woman. Feeling instantly protective, Daniel quickly removed his soaked shirt to cover her. "She's alive. She needs medical care." Daniel stated.

"Fine, take her below and lock her up." Charles casually commanded.

"She's been in the water for who knows how long," Daniel spat back, "She is nearly frozen and badly injured, she needs someplace warm, tools to clean her wounds, and a physician!" Daniel continued as he rubbed his hand along her arm to try to warm her icy skin. "We need to sterilize these gashes and stop at the nearest port."

"Not the rum!" a crew member had screeched in the crowd.

"Lock her up!" Charles once again demanded. "If you want to treat her, fine, but we are not making port to help this stranger we found in the sea. We don't even know who she is."

Knowing he could not win this battle, and needing to help the woman quickly, Daniel did as his father said and decided he would have to clean her wounds himself. After carrying her down to the cell, Daniel quickly went back to his quarters for supplies. He stripped his bed of his pillows and blankets to fashion a makeshift bed in her cell. He took a bottle of liquor from his own secret stash, a few old linens to use as bandages, and finally something for her to wear. Daniel had a few of his mother's old dresses, they may have been out of fashion, but he was sure she would not mind.

Clearing out a few damp and dirty rags from the cell, Daniel laid out a few blankets to make a nice thick layer to hopefully overcome the cold and hard wooden floor of the cell. Carefully laying the young woman on his makeshift bed, he began to clean her wounds. Pouring alcohol on to a rag, Daniel gently pressed on her open gashes. Surprisingly, most were not so deep and would probably heal in just a few days. There was only one that concerned him. Near The woman's shoulder, next to her collarbone, there was a large gash that looked as if she had been pierced straight through. Daniel softly wiped away the blood from the area to sanitize the wound. As his soft strokes continued, Daniel felt an icy hand grab his wrist.

"It's ok, you're safe now" Daniel assured the woman as he could see her eyes slowly flutter open, "I am just cleaning these gashes."

"Who are you?" the woman weakly asked as she squinted her eyes to try and focus her vision on Daniel.

"I'm Daniel, what's your name?"

"My name," the woman slowly started, "my name," was all she could say before once again passing out.

"It's ok, we can get to introductions later; you need your rest," Daniel said, not knowing if she could still actually hear him or not.

Bloody rags piled all around as Daniel continued to dress the wound. Finally, after almost every extra piece of linen and half the bottle of his rum, each wound was cleaned and wrapped. Seeing her weakened state, Daniel knew it was unnecessary to chain her wrists in the cuffs attached to the wall like other prisoners. She was not a threat, and Daniel did not want her to feel like a prisoner. Giving her space to rest, Daniel tucked her in and left the dress on the floor nearby, for her to dress into when or if she felt she could. Not happy about the idea of locking her in a cell, Daniel reluctantly did so as it was better than the alternative. Taking one last look at the unconscious woman, Daniel headed back to the deck to report to his father.

As Daniel approached the deck, all eyes were on him. Receiving a few nods and winks, he knew what kind of sick sadistic thoughts some of the men were probably thinking. *A pirate with a beautiful unconscious woman?* Daniel had hoped that most of the crew, even the newer ones, would know his character enough to know he would never do what they would have in a heartbeat. Daniel may have been a pirate, but he was not a scallywag, as they would say. Ignoring the gossip and chatter from the crew, Daniel approached his father.

"So, did she live?" Charles asked uncompassionately.

"Yes, I think she will be ok, just a few cuts here and there plus a bigger laceration on her shoulder. In a few days, I think she should heal fine." Daniel explained.

"Few days?" Charles sharply asked. "No, we do not have enough food to feed another mouth."

"Then she can have my portions." Daniel challenged.

"Fine, you can starve then." Charles answered coldly, "Besides, I guess it is not so horrible having her on board, a few of the men haven't enjoyed the company of a woman in their bed for quite some time…"

"No! I don't want any of these men touching her!" Daniel growled with a furious look taking over his face.

"You don't think these men deserve to have a little fun? What about that young man I threw overboard," Charles said as he pointed Peter out, "surely he deserves some fun after that. Bet he's still a virgin too."

"I will be the only one to watch over her!"

A slick smile formed on Charles's face. "Aye boy, I see," Charles replied as he gave Daniel a wink, "you want her all to yourself eh?"

"No, I just meant"-

"I understand," Charles said winking once again at his son, "Fine, you can keep her for now, but I have not changed my mind. She will remain locked in the cell. If you should need to feel relief, you will do it there, got it?"

Daniel quickly agreed, knowing it was the only way to get his father off the subject. If this is what it took to get him to let her stay, then so be it. Of course, he would never do what his father implied, but at least she would be safe from the other pirates. He could go along with the ruse for a few days, then when they made port, she would be free to safely go on her way.

Chapter 4

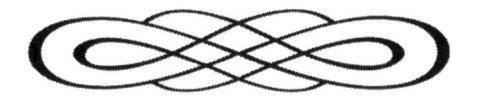

The ship sailed through the brisk night and Daniel found himself checking on the young woman almost every hour. She was still out cold during each check-up, but as he could see the blankets he bundled her in moving slowly up and down, he knew she was breathing peacefully. *Always a good sign,* he thought. As the night loomed on, and now with no rush to be anywhere, sleep shifts began. Worried that someone in the crew would accidentally "sleepwalk" down to her cell, Daniel thought it was best if he slept downstairs, just outside of her cell. Gathering some shirts and various other clothing items, Daniel set himself up a nest to sleep on. Laying on his side, his eyes fixated on the sleeping woman, Daniel slowly started to nod off.

Awoken by the sounds of screams, Daniel jolted up from his slumber. Assuming one of the men had snuck into her cell, Daniel instinctively drew his sword.

Observing the area, he realized there was no one there, just a frightened young woman in a cell who was finally awake. "Hey," Daniel said calmly, "It's alright, you are safe, I am not going to hurt you," he finished before putting away his sword.

"Where am I?" the woman asked quickly in a state of panic.

This introduction was not going well, Daniel thought. "I know you are in a cell, but believe me you are safe, I'm Daniel, what's your name?" he asked as he tried to keep his distance so as not to scare her further.

"Halianna," she responded, her voice still filled with fear.

Daniel slowly approached the cell, "I'm Daniel," he said calmly as he opened the door to join her inside, his hands up to show he meant no harm.

"Where am I? Why am I in a cage?" Halianna asked as she scanned her surroundings.

Slowly inching forward, Daniel said, "You are on a ship, we found you."

Before he could finish, she leaped towards him, grabbing ahold of the sword that hung on his side. She quickly defended herself and pointed to sword towards Daniel.

"Hey, let's calm down now." Daniel said gently, his hands still in the air as he could see the tip of his sword aimed straight toward his chest if he made the wrong move. "I am, nor is anyone on this ship going to harm you, you have my word."

Halianna stood there silent, observing the man at the mercy of her newly possessed sword. Just as she started to lower it, something caught her eye. Immediately, Halianna raised the sword back up and took a step closer. "I know you, you did this," she said using one hand to point at her various wounds. "I saw you."

"I found you in the water and I saved you," Daniel explained. "As I was dressing your wounds, you came to for a few seconds. Why would I rescue you from the water if my intent was to harm you?"

There was a long silence. Slowly she brought the sword down to her side. She kept a tight grip, but it was indeed lowered. Once again Halianna looked at her surroundings, then back to the man cowering in front of her. "So, if you saved me, why am I in this cell?" she asked sharply.

"My father, the captain of the ship, insisted. I know it is not ideal, but you must remain here if you are to remain on the ship."

"So I am a prisoner?" she shot back.

"No, not at all," Daniel began, "My father is not one to be crossed, and it was the only way to have him agree to let you stay on board. In a few days, when your wounds begin to heal and you gather back your strength, we will drop you off at a port."

Halianna took a moment to assess the severity of her wounds. Looking beneath her bandages at her freshly dressed wounds, it was evident that Daniel was telling the truth. Realizing Daniel was being honest, she handed him back his sword. "Thank you," Daniel said as he inserted the sword back into its sheath. "How did you become stranded in the ocean?"

"What?" she asked, her eyes fixated on every move Daniel made as he slowly stepped towards her.

"I found you clinging to a piece of wooden debris in the water, were you thrown from a boat or a ship nearby?"

"Yes," Halianna quickly replied. "I was on a ship, and we were fired upon, I went overboard."

"Thanks father," Daniel mumbled under his breath, "You must have been on the ship we fired at from the distance, I apologize for that. My father wanted to send the ship a message."

"What message was that?"

"We were on a fool's quest to find the sea serpent near the Isle of the Blessed, he was trying to mark his claim." Daniel shared with disgust in his voice.

"And did you find what you were looking for?" she innocently asked.

"No, no we didn't." Daniel lied. "Was that why you and your ship were out there Hali- what was it again?"

"Halianna, but Hali is fine." She replied with a small smile on her face. "Yes, and we were unsuccessful as well."

"I see." Daniel finished as he gazed at Hali. "Well, I need to attend to some business on deck, but I can bring you some food and water a little later. Next to your bed I left you something to wear."

Hali looked down at the dress he was referring to. She swiftly picked it up and observed the piece of fabric. It was a simple blue dress that was aged evident by its faded hue on the threadbare material. The dress being a better alternative to Daniel's damp shirt she had been wearing, Hali began to undress.

Daniel quickly turned his head to give her some privacy as he felt the heat creeping up his neck. "Um," Daniel said, slightly thrown by the intimacy of the moment, "Well, I will be back with some food in the morning," he said as he exited and locked her cell. Trying to hide his face, which was still flushed from seeing her, Daniel began to head up the steps.

"Daniel," Hali called out, causing Daniel to quickly turn back to her, "Thank you."

"You're welcome," Daniel replied, his gaze and smile lingering for just a brief moment snapping out of it and continuing up the stairs towards the deck.

Daniel needed to report back to his father about the new found state of the woman, of Hali. He would inform him that Hali was alive and would be okay to leave the ship in a few days. He figured it would be best if he left out the part where Hali had easily captured his own sword, leaving him at her mercy. That is something Charles would never let him live down. Plus it may hurt Hali's case if Charles knew she could use a sword just as well as any man. No need to raise those fears that would most definitely result in a negative outcome for her. It was settled; he would keep that part to himself.

Daniel began searching the deck for his father, but was interrupted by Felix and August on his mission. "So," Felix said teasingly, "How was it?"

"Yeah, did you have yourself some fun, Danny boy?" August added as he started to jab at Daniel with his elbow.

"Ha ha, really funny you two." Daniel responded, "No, we were asleep most of the time..."

"Did you tire each other out, if you know what I mean?" Felix winked.

"Asleep on opposite sides of the cell," Daniel firmly added. "Nothing happened, but she is awake now and it looks like she will be just fine."

August and Felix shot each other a glance, unconvinced of Daniel's story. With that, they both quietly nodded towards one another and dispersed back to their positions on the ship. Clearing the way, Daniel could see his father straight ahead working on a map. Daniel bee-lined towards his father, ready to fill him in on his findings.

"Well, she lived through the night?" Charles nonchalantly asked, still focused on the task at hand.

"Yes, her name is Hali and she should heal up just fine." Daniel stated. "So, when do we make port?"

"Not sure yet, Maybe a day or two, depending."

"Depending on what?" Daniel asked.

"Well, looking at this map, if we start heading north now, it appears we can find a town off the shores of Ireland. Haven't explored that area too much just yet. Could be a good opportunity." Charles pointed out the island on the map.

"That is a pretty quiet spot, or so I have been told. The chances of there being a doctor for Hali there are pretty slim."

"So? You said she was alive, why does she need a doctor?" Charles asked, lacking any compassion in his tone.

"I just thought..."

"That was your first mistake," Charles asserted, "We will drop her off when we can, but for now, she is on our time. End of discussion."

He'd rather not anger his father any further, especially when considering the thin line he was already walking on their relationship. As much as Daniel wanted to get Hali somewhere safe, he could not help but selfishly be a little happy. More days meant more opportunities to know her a little more. Being his father's son, it was always work, work, work. There was never any time to meet a nice young lady. *Maybe this girl could be the one?* Daniel thought to himself. Sailing on, he still could not shake the vision of Hali from his mind. As much as he tried, his thoughts constantly trailed off and made their way back to Hali. Thoughts that left a small remaining smile on his young face until sunrise.

Another long night had passed, and although Daniel was exhausted, the sunrise meant it was a new morning. And a new morning meant it was time for breakfast. Daniel prepared a plate for Hali using his portions from what would have been his meal. On the cleanest plate he could find, he added some bread, fresh fruit of grapes and an apple, and a few slabs of ham. It was nothing luxurious, but he was sure she must have been hungry enough to eat just about anything. Tucking in his shirt and brushing back his wild, wind blown hair, Daniel cast one last glance in the mirror before heading down to the cells.

Daniel slowly crept down the stairs, trying his best to avoid the steps that were just a bit too squeaky, in case Hali was still asleep. With a deep breath, Daniel reached the last step, rounding the corner towards her cell.

Looking through the bars, he could see she was tucked in and asleep. Lingering for just a moment, Daniel figured it was probably best not to wake her. He quietly opened the cell door and left the plate of food on the floor nearby Hali's temporary bed. He took one final glance at the sleeping maiden before locking the cell back up and heading out.

"Daniel?" A soft and sleepy voice called out. "What are you doing?"

Daniel turned to face the now awake Hali. He had tried his best to be quiet, but she had stirred anyways. "Good morning, sorry to wake you I just brought you down some breakfast." Daniel finished as he pointed out the plate next to her. "I'll let you eat in peace." He finished as he started to leave.

"Wait," Hali called out. "I wouldn't mind the company, if you wanted to stay."

He beamed. "Sure, I can stay." Rejoining Hali in her cell, Daniel plopped down on the floor. After a few moments of silence, Daniel figured he should probably say something. "So, how do you feel?" Daniel inquired, breaking the silence.

"Still in pain, but feeling much better." Hali popped a grape in her mouth. "When will we be making port?"

"Um, about that," he paused. "I am not entirely sure, we may be making a quick stop before we reach a town, so for now you will have to stay here." Daniel said a little nervously.

Hali stopped eating as her face turned to worry. "How much longer?" Hali asked concerned.

"Hopefully no more than a few days," Daniel answered, trying to put her at ease. "But don't worry, you will be safe down here and I promise you will always have a meal."

"I suppose I don't have a choice." Hali said, reluctantly taking a bite of the piece of ham. "Where is your breakfast?"

Daniel wasn't sure if he should lie and say he had eaten already, or just tell her the truth that the meal she was currently enjoying was his own. He decided it was best to not add to her worries and have her feel any kind of guilt. "I ate already, quite full in fact." Daniel lied as he patted his belly. "So what were you doing on the other ship, the one you were thrown from?" Daniel asked, hoping to make conversation.

"Uh, it was a trading ship. I was just onboard for the ride, and got caught up in the mess. They were not the nicest of men."

Daniel nodded in agreement. Most men at sea only wanted a woman onboard for personal pleasures. Beyond that, it was typically not fit for a woman. Sea life was a difficult one, one that very few could handle. *She must have been tough,* Daniel thought. "I can't say the men on this ship are any different, to be honest." Daniel admitted.

Hali stared back at Daniel as she paused from popping another grape in her mouth. "But you are. Are you not?" She asked.

Daniel had always considered himself to be better than most of the men who have come and gone throughout the years on the Grey Siren. However, guilt resurfaced anytime something bad happened at the commands of his father and he had done nothing to stop it. He may not have been the one doing it, but he also hadn't stopped it, just like the situation Hali was now in. He may have made her comfortable, but she was still in a cell. She was still being treated like a common prisoner.

"I try to be." Daniel answered quietly.

"I'm alive because of you, never forget that," she paused before adding, "I know I won't." Hali added as she reached her hand out to grab his.

Daniel's face could not hide how he felt. He felt it all, the blood rushing to his cheeks, the fluttering in his stomach, the heat radiating off of his skin. He inhaled slowly before turning away to hide his flushed face.

"Are you alright?" Hali asked as she saw Daniel turn away.

"Yes, sorry." Daniel replied as he slowly turned back towards Hali, hoping his face had turned to a normal color again. "I see the dress fits." Daniel said, trying to get the attention off of himself.

"Yes, it does, thank you. Who's was it anyways?" Hali asked as she pulled on the dress to make it more neat and clean. "I thought you didn't have women aboard?"

Daniel paused for a moment as he saw Hali standing there, looking breathtaking in his mother's dress. He wasn't sure if he should bring up that painful chapter in his life. Looking at Hali's sapphire eyes, gazing back at him, her long silver hair framing her body and the dress that brought back fond memories, he figured there was no harm in telling her. "It was my mother's actually." Daniel sadly replied, preparing himself for the inevitable conversation that was soon to follow.

"Oh," Hali stated as she saw Daniels face, "Is she on the ship as well?" she asked softly.

"No, she died I am afraid. About eleven years ago."

"I am so sorry, what happened?" Hali said as she took a step towards Daniel.

"Influenza. You see, she stayed home with me while my father was out with the Grey Siren doing, well, living his life of piracy." Daniel started to slink to the floor as he looked down. "He was always gone, and I watched her get sicker and sicker each day. We wrote to my father, but by the time he came home it was too late." Daniel finished as he felt a tear roll down his cheek.

Hali joined Daniel on the floor. "So young to experience so much tragedy. How did you father take it?"

"Not well," Daniel replied as he wiped the tear away, "He has never been a nice man, but that was the day he truly became an evil man, it was like the last thing keeping his humanity was taken away."

"What about you? His son, wasn't that enough?"

"I wish," Daniel said as he turned his face to meet Hali's saddened eyes. "That day, he emotionally disconnected from everyone, even me. I was just to carry out the family name and legacy by being the next captain of the Grey Siren, nothing more."

Hali reached out and took hold of Daniel's hand. A wave of calm passed over him as he felt the warmth of her skin on his as their fingers intertwined. Feeling his heart beating faster, he had hoped Hali could not hear it, as it felt like it would burst from his own chest. Sitting there, comforted by another human being was something Daniel was not used to. It was something he did not know he needed until he had it. Letting her go would be hard Daniel thought. For now, he would just need to enjoy the moment.

Breaking the silence, Daniel stood up, "I have an idea." Daniel exclaimed. "I think you should meet my father for dinner."

Hali slowly stood up with a confused look on her face, "Meet your father? Isn't he a horrid person, I mean from everything you have said, it just seems like that is not the best idea."

"Maybe if he sees how kind you are, and that you are not a threat, well, maybe he will understand that we should get you on land sooner than later." Daniel vocalized as his mind was still formulating an idea. "He may even let you out of the cell."

"Alright, I will give it a try." Hali said sweetly with doubt in her voice.

The two continued to talk as Hali finished her breakfast. They swapped stories about the different sights they have seen throughout the world and the life experiences that came with it. Daniel could tell Hali was still a bit hesitant in letting her guard down, even in front of Daniel, so he did most of the talking. This didn't bother him one bit, it was nice to just talk, especially about things other than sailing, treasure, and piracy. The sound above indicated that the crew was up and it was time to get to work. Taking Hali's dishes, Daniel headed up the steps to get the day started. He would wait for the right time to spring the question on his father about having an extra guest for dinner.

Chapter 5

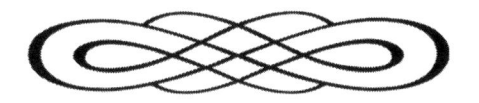

The sun shone brightly in the blue sky as the ship carried on towards its next location. Daniel looked out at the sea with a peaceful smile sweeping across his face. Taking in a deep breath, the sea air filling his lungs, Daniel was actually in a chipper mood that was different from his usual dread of the monotonous day of sailing. The waves seemed to crash against the ship in a melodic tone on this morning, bringing music to Daniel's ears. As he observed the crew all partaking in their positions, Daniel caught sight of Charles at the helm focused on the sea as usual. With a bit of a dance in his step, Daniel headed towards his father.

"Well," Charles started as Daniel approached, "Is that a smile I see? Looks like someone had an enjoyable morning." Charles finished as he shot his son a wink.

Rather than telling his father the truth about their innocent conversation, he decided to go with it. The last thing Daniel needed was more pushback from his father, especially when he needed him to agree to a dinner. If she could make a good impression on Charles, maybe he would be more lenient about her presence on board.

"Yes, Father, it was a wonderful morning and I will take that to the grave." Daniel replied, as he winked back to keep up the ruse.

His lie seemed to put his father in good spirits. *Had this been the secret to making him proud of his son this whole time?* Daniel thought to himself as his father began to tease and joke around about Daniel's morning of "shaking in the sheets." As long as it kept his father in a good mood, he would play along. Daniel began to give his father some more bawdy and vulgar conversation about his morning, hoping his real life inexperience wouldn't show. Hoping not to get caught in the lie, Daniel tried to keep his descriptions fairly general and pulled from stories he had heard from other sailors in the past. So far it seemed to work.

"So," said Charles, taking a swig from a bottle of rum, "be honest Danny boy. Was she your first?" he finished, offering the bottle to Daniel.

Taking a small sip, Daniel replied, "Yes, all the way at least."

"That's my boy!" Charles yelled, slapping his son in the back. "You know, you could keep her for a bit if you'd like, just until you're done with her."

Daniel tried to hide his quick turn to anger after hearing these words. He hated the way his father talked about Hali. He even hated the lies he told to convince his father of his sexual experience with her, but this hit a nerve. He knew his father was not fond of romance of any kind since the passing of his mother, but the fact was that he now just saw women as objects, something to be used and discarded. In moments like this, he couldn't help but think of his father as truly nothing but a crude rogue. Still, he had to keep up the act to maintain the positive energy in the air. "No, I think I will let this one go when we make port in the next village, maybe find myself another. One who isn't covered in gashes." Daniel replied, trying to match his father's sleazy tone.

"I'm sure those cuts caused some limitations, but don't worry, you will find a better one."

Trying to steer the conversation another direction, Daniel attempted to muster up the courage to ask his father about dinner. Seeing that Charles had drank just about half the bottle of rum that was attached to his hand, causing him to be three sheets to the wind, he figured his chances were getting better. Maybe a few more friendly comments would help. "Father if I may, I would like to talk more about my role as a captain once you retire." He ventured, hoping his father would take the bait.

"You do? Well this is a change, let us talk."

"I was thinking over dinner perhaps." Daniel replied, trying to tip-toe carefully to the question.

"I thought you were giving your food rations to that wench of yours?" Charles added.

Daniel smirked a bit as he realized his plan of turning the conversation towards dinner was working. Charles had taken the bait to follow him exactly where Daniel wanted him. "Oh you are right Father. After all, I need her to keep her energy up if you know what I mean," Daniel chuckled as he jabbed his father with his elbow. "Perhaps, the girl could dine with us?"

"Dine with us?" Charles repeated with a bit of irritation in his voice.

"Yes, that way maybe you can give me your opinion of her. After all, if I decide to keep Hali, I'd love to know what you think of her." Daniel interjected as he waited for his father's reply.

Daniel stared at his father, hoping he would accept. He could see Charles looking out to the sea as the cogs turned in his drunken head. "Well…" Charles began, before Daniel chimed in with one last comment.

"Also, I think hearing us talk about my future status will surely impress her."

"Fine, but you must keep your eyes on her at all times. If she steps out of line, it will be the plank for her!" Charles declared as he pointed towards the sea.

The thought of seeing Hali walk the plank and to be left to drown made Daniel feel uneasy. Daniel had seen countless men chained and tied up with bricks as they walked the short walk to their watery deaths. Each one made Daniel emotional in the past, he could not begin to understand how he would feel if he saw Hali on the end on the plank, to be lost in the sea forever. He had to think positive thoughts. At least his father agreed though, and if this went well, it could mean she would be let out of the cell. Possibly even free to roam and not feel like the prisoner she was. Plus, with August and Felix there, maybe he would be on a bit better behavior than usual. Maybe a woman on board was just the thing his father needed. It sure was for Daniel. *It just had to go well,* Daniel thought as he already started to think of ways to prep Hali to ensure his idea would work.

Charles seemed to be in good spirits as they sailed through the day. Not one single crew member aggravated him, nor did he yell at any of the men. This change in attitude could not had been timed more perfectly. Maybe the thought of his son's sexual encounter now deemed him a man, one to be proud of. Or maybe the fact that Daniel was finally accepting his fate as the future captain of the Grey Siren altered his mood. Either way, the day was a pleasant one, one that would hopefully lead into a pleasant night.

As the sun began to set, it signaled that dinner shifts would soon begin. Wanting to get a head start on the preparations, Daniel dismissed himself to his father's quarters early. Making the place a little tidier then normal,

Daniel hustled to clean up the very lived in space. Tucking away his father's soiled clothing as well as the few loose pistols and swords laying about. After discarding of the many empty bottles of rum and wine that were scattered around, the place was actually shaping up to look descent enough to have a lady join them for dinner. Now to check on the food.

Daniel made his way to the galley where Peter was on chef duty for the night. From what Daniel could see, Peter had very little knowledge around a galley as well as being a chef in any capacity. He had to save this poor man. "Need a little help?" Daniel asked as he started to tie an apron that was in need of a wash around his waist, "You look a little overwhelmed."

"The captain put me on cooking duty," Peter said as his hands shook, "and I'm afraid if he doesn't like what I make, well, I am afraid he will throw me overboard again."

"Don't worry, I'll take care of it, you go ahead and go to your sleeping quarters for now, and in about an hour, come check on it and serve us in the captain's quarters. It will be our little secret." Daniel said as he ushered Peter out.

"Thank you sir!" Peter exclaimed as he exited the galley.

Daniel looked around to see what kind of meal he could whip up. There wasn't much to work with, but he wanted Hali to have the best meal possible. All but a few apples of the fresh fruit and vegetables had now gone bad and there was only a small amount of salted meat left. It seemed it would be time to do some fishing soon to restock on food, but for now, he figured, the salted meat would have to do, as long as he could cook it right.

Growing up with his mother, Daniel learned his way around a kitchen and how to cook with the bare essentials. Daniel started searching through every cabinet for food that would suffice as a side and luckily he found a few loaves of bread that had not yet turned stale. *This would have to do,* Daniel thought as he prepared their meals for the evening. Daniel threw the meat into the metal box in the kitchen and lit the sand below to begin the cooking process. It would take a bit until it was fully cooked, but that gave him enough time to prep Hali on how to act and what to say, or rather what not to say.

With dinner cooking, Daniel made his way towards his sleeping quarters. The dress which he had provided Hali was not built for warmth, and with the walk from the cells to the captain's quarters, the air could get quite frigid. Not having any other dress options, Daniel dug around his wardrobe chest for a robe or cape of some sort. It wouldn't compliment her looks, but it would keep her warm. Reaching the bottom of the chest, Daniel found the crimson cape he had not worn for years. It was a little moth eaten like most clothing in his chest, and it was very wrinkled, but much like the state of everything else on the ship, it would have to do. Bundling the cape under his arm, Daniel made his way back to the kitchen to check on dinner, then towards Hali's cell.

Walking down the steps Daniel whispered "Hali, it's me," as not to startle her. Seeing that she was awake, Daniel proceeded towards her cell and let himself in.

"Well?" Hali asked as she watched Daniel enter her cell, "What did he say?"

"Surprisingly, he said yes. But I need to kind of warn you of a few things."

"What?"

"Well, he agreed to have you join us for dinner because he thinks we," Daniel paused. Clearing is throat, "He thinks we are," embarrassed to say the words in front of a lady, Daniel could only bring himself to make awkward motions with his hands as he brought them together in almost a round of applause sort.

"Oh," Hali stated, realizing that he meant sex, "Oh, I see."

"You do?"

"I mean, whatever it was you were doing with your hands is not quite accurate, but I understood what you were trying to say." Hali paused before asking him the question that was now on her mind. "Um, have you ever," she inquired as she mimicked his hand gestures from before, "with a woman?"

Turning red and once again feeling embarrassed, Daniel turned away from Hali. He wasn't sure what to say. He figured he may not ever see Hali again, so the truth couldn't hurt. Turning back to face Hali, who had now stepped closer to him, he answered, "No, no I have not."

"I figured," Hali said with a light giggle under her breath.

"Have you?" Daniel asked as he took a step closer to Hali.

"With only one man, but it was a very long time ago," Hali said as she let her eyes wander to the floor, "It is a time I would like to forget." Bringing her eyes back to meet Daniels, "So, what other things do I need to know before I walk into the shark pit."

"Well, he is going to size you up, see if you are worth keeping around."

"I thought I was going to be free to go once I've healed?" Hali quickly vocalized.

"You will, but if he likes you and trusts you, he will let you out of the cell and you will be free to roam the ship and rest in my sleeping quarters." Daniel explained, trying to reassure her.

"You're sleeping quarters?" Hali asked suspiciously.

"Yes, but I am a gentleman and you may have the bed, I can take the floor, trust me I have slept on worse. Deal?" Daniel said as he held his hand out for a shake.

"Alright, deal." Hali replied as she placed her hand his, giving it a firm shake.

Daniel continued to explain to Hali how to behave and act in the presence of the captain. Agreeing to be on her best behavior and to be as Daniel put it, "his perfect little wench," Hali understood the plan. Act coy and charming, be submissive, and don't start a fight. Any disagreement could cost Hali her life.

"Oh, here," Daniel said, remembering the cape he had picked out for her, "It can get a little chilly when walking about the ship."

"Thank you." She replied as she began to put on the cape, struggling to tie it in the front.

"Here," Daniel chuckled, "let me help you." Daniel reached his hands out and began to tie the top of the cape together. His hands just below her neck. He could feel her warm breath on his fingers as Hali looked down at Daniel's rough hands as he fastened the lace in front. As he was finishing, Hali and Daniel both looked up in unison, their eyes locking on each other. Daniel knew what he wanted to do, he wanted to plant a soft kiss on her pink lips while his hands framed her satin skin. Lost in his own thoughts while still staring into Hali's sparkling eyes, something unexpected happened.

Hali reached her hands towards Daniel's unshaven face, cupping each side of his cheeks as she lowered his face to meet hers. Breathing rapidly, Hali pressed her lips against his. Daniel could taste her sweet breath as his lips naturally knew what to do. Instinctively, Daniel placed his hands onto Hali's shoulders, causing her to wince in pain and take a step back.

"I'm sorry," Daniel said apologetically, "I just got carried away; I didn't mean to hurt you."

"No, I'm the one who is sorry. I don't know what came over me." Hali said, raising one hand to her forehead, the other on her shoulder where her bandage-covered wound was.

"Are you alright?"

"I'll be fine," Hali said as she tried to crack a reassuring smile as she lowered her hand from her shoulder.

Both were now red in the face and flustered. Daniel wanted more, but figured it was best to move on and continue on with their dinner plans. He didn't want to let himself get carried away again. Wanting to put an end to the awkward air that now loomed over them both, Daniel spoke up. "Shall we head to dinner?" Daniel said, clearing his throat.

"We shall," Hali answered as she composed herself.

The chill in the air had a bite to it. *Good thing I grabbed her the cape*, Daniel thought as he looked down at Hali, holding her arms together to stay warm, shivering rhythmically. They continued with urgency towards the captain's quarters where warmth was sure to be and a hot meal would be waiting for them.

Rounding the corner, the two headed down the stairs to Charles' private quarters. As they entered, Daniel took a look around, but August and Felix were nowhere in sight, just his father sitting comfortably at the end of the table, sipping from a chalice. Approaching the room with caution in fear of a trap, Daniel guided Hali behind him for safety. "Where are August and Felix?" Daniel asked, still slowly entering the room.

"I thought you were here to have dinner with me Danny boy, so we could talk." Charles replied with a twinge of irritation in his voice.

Swallowing hard, Daniel tried to lighten the mood, "Of course, it's just that, well they are always here, but this works out much better." Daniel stated with a fake smile filling his face.

"Well," Charles said as he took a large gulp from his chalice, "Don't hide her, behind ya' boy, let's see her."

Daniel looked back at Hali and gave her a reassuring look as he nodded to her. Taking her hand, Daniel guided Hali towards the front of him to face Charles, who was still relaxed in his seat across the room. Daniel could feel Hali squeezing his hand, causing him to jump in. "Father, this is Hali, Hali, this is my Father." Daniel said as he referenced Charles.

"Eh, did we leave something out Danny boy?" Charles vainly added.

"Sorry, Hali, this is the notorious pirate, Charles the Dread, captain of the Grey Siren, feared throughout the seven seas." Daniel announced as proudly as possible.

Hali nervously curtsied towards Charles' direction as Charles got out of his chair and started to head her way. Intensely watching, Daniel didn't move as his eyes followed his father's movements, until he stood right in front of Hali.

"Does she talk?" Charles rudely asked.

Clearing her throat, Hali spoke up, "Yes, she does." Hali nervously replied, "It's a pleasure to meet you Captain Charles."

"You caused quite a stir the other day," Charles said, his voice deep and intense, "if it were up to me, I would have left you in the sea to feed the fishes, but Daniel here, he had other plans for you. Make sure you let him know how thankful you are." Charles said menacingly as his eyes traced Hali's body.

"Father, that's enough." Daniel quietly added.

"I'm just jesting Danny boy!" Charles exclaimed as he took another sip from his chalice. "Come, sit and we shall get this evening started. Dinner should be out soon."

Charles led the way towards the table with Daniel and Hali just behind him. Daniel pulled out a chair for Hali before sitting down on his own. Taking a deep breath, Daniel let his tense body relax just a bit. Just as he let his muscles soften, the sound of his father's loud drunken voice put Daniel back on his guard. *What now?* Daniel thought, hoping his father was not too drunk, passing from a happy mood to a foul one.

"This is a proper dinner, take off that cape!" Charles demanded.

"She is just warming herself up, she will have it off before dinner is served." Daniel explained.

"No, my table my rules, take it off." Charles intensely replied.

Taking a deep breath of frustration in, Daniel got up from his chair to take Hali's cape. Daniel placed his hands along her neck again as he untied the lace keeping the cape closed. Once the knot was free, Daniel placed the cape on the backside of her chair, all the while, Charles eyes were fixated on Hali.

"What are you wearing?" Charles said slowly through his clenched teeth.

"It's a dress sir, surely it is proper enough for your dinner." Hali responded with a hint of disdain and sarcasm in her voice.

"Daniel," Charles yelled, pounding his fist on the table as he flew up from his chair, "What is that wench doing wearing your mother's dress.

Daniel began to feel flooded with panic. He did not think his father would even recognize or remember that dress. With Charles now charging towards Hali, Daniel knew he had to mediate and calm down the situation. This was what he was afraid of. "Father, I did not think you would even remember it." Daniel said apologetically as he wedged himself between Hali and his father. "I am sorry, it is my fault. I am the one who gave her the dress, she had no idea of its origins."

"Take it off now!" Charles screamed as he looked past his son, straight into Hali's fearful eyes.

"Fine" Daniel interjected, "just let me go to my cabin and grab her something of mine to wear."

"No," Charles replied as he pushed Daniel aside and stepped closer to Hali who was now shaking with fear, "take it off now, I will not ask again!"

"Please just let me," Daniel started.

"No, now or I will cut it off of her flesh." Charles said as he withdrew his sword. "And that may not be the only thing I cut."

Daniel watched as his father's sword was aimed right at Hali. He wished he could save Hali from the shame and embarrassment of being forced to strip of her clothes. He never could have imagined his father would react in such a way. *This was a bad idea,* Daniel thought to himself as he felt the guilt creeping in for even suggesting this plan. He and Hali shared a look, he knew she was looking to him for help, a service he could not provide at the moment. Shifting his eyes towards the ground, Daniel nodded his head for her to comply with his father's orders.

"Can she at least put back on the cape?" Daniel asked, his eyes and neck still anchored towards the floorboards.

"No, she shall freeze and dine just the way we found her, in the nude." Charles cruelly replied.

With a tear rolling down her cheek, Hali did as Charles ordered and slowly removed the dress. With a quick motion, Charles snatched the dress straight out of her arms, all the while Daniel helplessly stood in his place and watched. The room was quiet for a moment, perhaps a moment too long in anticipation of what would happen next.

"That's a good girl," Charles said with a smug look on his face as he looked Hali up and down, "Now where were we?" Charles stated as he turned back towards his chair, "Oh that's right!" Charles exclaimed as he whipped back around, slapping Hali clean across the face with such force, it caused her to fall towards the floor, her silver hair completely whipped to one side.

"Father!" Daniel yelled as he started to rush towards Hali to help her.

"You stay right where you are or you are next," Charles threatened as he towered over Hali's limp body on the floor. "Now little missy," Charles started before he noticed something that stopped him mid-sentence. Looking down at Hali, Charles caught sight of something he did not notice before. Along her spine, where Hali's long hair usually was draped over, something caught Charles' vision.

"It can't be," Charles' silently said to himself in astonishment as he lowered his sword.

Regaining her strength, Hali lunged forward, using all her weight to tackle Charles' down. Seizing his sword, Hali pointed it straight at Charles throat as he crawled along the floor.

"Hali don't!" Daniel cried out.

"Why not, he is an evil man, you said it yourself." Hali replied, her eyes and attention still focused on Charles and the aim of her sword.

Approaching with caution, Daniel slowly joined Hali by her side. He had to deescalate the situation and fast. If she kills Charles, the crew would surely be out for blood, especially Felix and August. If she surrendered,

Charles would surely kill her. There was only one option, Daniel needed to get that sword and talk his father and Hali both down. There was no need for bloodshed.

"Hali, listen to me, if you kill this man, it will not end well for you, I promise you that." Daniel calmly explained.

"So you are on his side!" Hali cried out as she backed up, turning her attention towards both Daniel and Charles. Slowly retreating towards the steps, sword still in hand, Hali's breath became rapid. She was running out of options. As she was about to reach the first step, she heard Charles call out.

"Get her lad!" Charles screamed as Peter came down the stairs, ready to serve the dinner,

Doing as he was instructed and catching Hali off guard, Peter dropped the food and tackled Hali to the floor. As Daniel watched, he immediately began to rush to help Hali, but not before being pulled to the floor by Charles. While Hali and Peter wrestled on the floor, she lost hold of the sword, her only protection. Peter quickly grabbed it and with the hilt of the sword, he struck her with a strong blow to the head, rendering her unconscious. Just as he was about to strike and finish her off, Charles shouted- "No! Do not kill her!" Charles screamed as he pulled himself up from the floor, "We need her alive."

With confusion of his father's decision echoing in his ear, Daniel quickly brought himself to his feet. He rushed over to see Hali still pinned to the floor by peter as Charles pulled some rope from a drawer. "What is going on?" Daniel asked as he watched his father tie Hali up.

"This," Charles said as he flipped Hali's lifeless body over, revealing a large tattoo that ran along her spine.

"So, she has a tattoo?" Daniel replied, still confused at the situation.

"Not just any tattoo Danny boy, this is the map, the map to the fabled treasure of wonders!" Charles finished as he ran his hands along Hali's back.

Uncomfortable at the sight of his father touching her bare body, Daniel tried to compose himself and make sense of what his father was trying to explain. "I thought it was on the back of a sea serpent, not an innocent woman." Daniel shot back.

"Don't you see? This *is* the sea serpent. The beast must be able to take other forms," Charles explained as he and Peter finished tying her up. "When we blasted it, maybe we caused it to take a weaker form."

Going through all the events that led to finding Hali in the water, it all seem to make since. Her injuries must have been from the shots of the cannons. The large gaping hole below her shoulder must have been, *oh no, right where I stabbed the serpent,* Daniel thought as he put the pieces together. This lead Daniel to wonder if her kindness towards him was all an act, was she just waiting to get her revenge on him for stabbing her through? These were all thoughts Daniel decided to put aside as he watched Peter pick up the bound Hali. "What are you going to do with her?" Daniel asked, his voice full of worry.

"We will put her back in her cell, follow the map, and then dispose of the creature." Charles bluntly stated.

"Kill her? But once you find the treasure, why can't you just let her go?" Daniel urgently asked.

"You saw what it did to me, what it did to you! It's a wild animal, one that can't be let to be left alive, especially after its little dinner stunt."

"Her." Daniel quietly mumbled.

"What was that?"

"Her, she is not some beast or creature, she was a frightened young woman who only became that way after you humiliated and violated her!"

"Yes, yes I did, and do you want to know why," Charles said menacingly as he took a step towards Daniel, "Because you were right, I am an evil man." Charles finished as he started to follow Peter up the steps.

Overtaken by anger Daniel, reached up and grabbed the back of his father's vest, hurling him down the steps onto the floor. Daniel quickly composed himself as he started to race up the steps to stop Peter. Peter was only a few yards ahead as Daniel ran as quickly as he could. He didn't have a plan, he just knew he had to get Hali back. Maybe jump into the water with her and make a swim for it, he wasn't sure. The one thing he was sure of though, he had to reach her. "Peter, stop!" Daniel cried out as he picked up the pace.

A shot rang out, causing Daniel's ears to buzz and ring with pain as he collapsed to the ground. As he tried to recover from the pain in his ears, he looked down at his leg and could see the red liquid pouring out, glistening under the moonlight. Daniel looked back to try and identify where the shot came from. His vision dizzy from the pain, he could make out a figure. It was his father, holding a pistol, still looming with smoke from the blast. "You gave me no choice boy," Charles said as he approached Daniel.

Daniel tried to stand, but it was useless with the slug in his leg. Looking forward, he could no longer see Peter. He had failed. The commotion caused all eyes of the crew to be on Charles as he continued to point his pistol in Daniel's direction. "Felix, August!" Charles hollered.

"Captain." They responded in unison.

"Get some rope and tie this traitor up!" Charles ordered.

"Captain?" August responded as he and Felix glanced at each other then back to Daniel, still bleeding out on the ship deck. "Did you have a bit too much wine? That's Danny boy you just shot!"

"No, he is a traitor who would rather see his father sent to his grave, then some creature!" Charles screamed, his face turning red, "Now tie him up or you will be catching the next bullet!"

August and Felix grabbed some rope and joined Charles. With the pistol still aimed at Daniel, Daniel had no choice but to cooperate. "Don't do this," Daniel pleaded with Felix and August, "He is going to kill her!"

"Sorry Danny boy," Felix said with regret in his voice, "Captain's orders."

Tying Daniel's hands behind his back, they helped him to his feet. Finally up, Daniel could not help but let out a painful scream as his weight pressed down on his gunshot wound. Flinching from Daniels blood curdling screams, August turned towards Charles. "Are you sure this is necessary Captain?" August asked.

"Absolutely, you know that wench he saved from the water?" Charles asked as he was excited to share what he knew, "Turns out, she is not simply a helpless woman after all."

"What do you mean?" Felix chimed in.

"She is the beast, the sea serpent. They are one and the same!"

"Captain are you..." Felix started.

"I saw the tattoo on its back! The markings on the woman's back are the same as those on that faded piece of parchment I have. It's the markings on the serpent. We can use her to find the treasure of wonders!" Charles said in an upbeat tone. "Daniel was ready to let her go, or maybe even find the treasure all for himself!"

"Is it true?" August asked in disbelief as he faced Daniel.

"Yes," Daniel replied with pain in his voice, "But I did not know what she was, that I swear to you, because if I did, I would have tried to let her go long before!"

"See boys, he's nothing but a traitor! Now lock him up!"

Felix and August supported Daniel's weight the best they could as they marched him towards the prison cells below, being careful of his bullet ridden leg. The air was quiet as the rest of the crew stood in place, silently witnessing all of the events that had taken place in the matter of minutes. At the powerful sound of Charles' voice commanding everyone to get back to work, the crew nervously went about their business.

Chapter 6

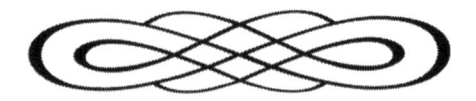

Arriving at the cell, Daniel could see Peter starting to exit as he had fulfilled his duty in locking up the unconscious and bound Hali in her cell. Felix and August placed Daniel into the cell directly across. His cell was much smaller due to Hali's cell being the modified model when the crew thought they would be boarding a sea serpent. The cell had not been cleaned in sometime as Daniel scanned the dirt floor. Dust everywhere and even a few bones from prior prisoners that did not make it out.

"I am sorry to do this Daniel," Felix started as he began unlocking the iron cuffs that hung along the wall, "But Captain's orders." August and Felix hoisted Daniel up as they started to secure each of his wrists to the hanging shackles. Too tired and in too much pain to even try to fight, Daniel let the men do their job without a fuss. Knowing that even if he were to best the two men, he wouldn't get too far with a bullet in his leg. Letting out a small grunt of pain as the men brought him to his feet yet again, Daniel was defeated. He was injured and shackled to the wall in a locked cell with no escape. Watching August and Felix heading to Hali's cell to do the same, Daniel had to try and reason with the men.

"Chain me up all you want, but just untie her and let her remain in the locked cell." Daniel pleaded.

"We can't let her even have a chance to escape Danny," August started as he began to untie Hali from the ropes she was secured in, "If she is in fact what the Captain says, we need her."

"She's been on this ship for a few days now, with no chains and ropes, just a locked cell, and not once has she been able to escape." Daniel replied as he tried to reason with the men.

"Things have changed, I am sorry." August finished as he placed each of Hali's wrists into the shackles that matched Daniel's.

"Before you chain her, can you just cover her please, my shirt should still be in her cell," Daniel said as he struggled to point out his shirt he had previous given her bundled on the floor.

Felix nodded and placed the oversized shirt onto Hali, covering up most of her naked body. After chaining Hali in the shackles, the two men departed, flashing Daniel an apologetic expression before heading back up the steps to the deck. Through the limited light provided, Daniel stared at Hali's limp body hanging from her iron restraints. Hearing nothing but the sea as the waves hit the hulls of the ship, Daniel tried to wake her. "Hali?" Daniel whispered loudly, hoping no one was standing guard just outside the door. "Hali, can you hear me?" Daniel tried again, but no response.

Time had passed as things above deck had gotten quieter and quieter as sleep shifts began. Daniel tried everything to break free from his shackles. Using all of his remaining strength to push his arms forward, trying to twist the chains, and even trying to slip his hands through, but was unsuccessful in each endeavor. *No prisoner in the past had ever broken free, so how can I?* Daniel thought as he grew tired from each attempt, his wrists now cut and scraped from the iron cuffs. Giving in to his situation, Daniel decided not to fight it. He began to close his eyes, hoping to slip into a deep sleep, anything to stop the pain and hopelessness of his present situation. Just as he started to slip away into dreamland, a place where the pain of his leg and arms did not exist, he heard a small noise from across the room and from the cell opposite of his.

"Hali?" Daniel whispered. "Are you awake?" Daniel could see small movements from Hali's cell as her head rocked back and forth, accompanied by small groans. Squinting his eyes to see in the darkness, Daniel caught sight of Hali's head pop up as she straightened her neck,

"D-Daniel?" Hali said softly in a dazed state. "What happened?" she finished as she started to realize her situation, pulling her arms against her chains.

"They chained us, both of us," Daniel responded with disdain in his voice.

"Why?" Hali responded with fear in her voice. "Why did they take you too?"

"Because I tried to save you from my father when he found out what you really are." Daniel stated as he waited for a reply. "Is it true?"

"Is what true?" Hali asked as innocently as possible.

Daniel took a deep breath in. He didn't want to outright accuse her of deceiving him, of deceiving everyone. For all he knew, there could be another explanation as to why she has the same markings of the sea serpent. Even if it were true, and she and the serpent are one and the same, that didn't mean she was planning on killing him was it? So many thoughts raced through his mind as Daniel tried to find the right words to uncover the truth. "Are you human?" Daniel asked realizing how silly he must have sounded, "I mean, are you the sea serpent, the one we were hunting?"

Hali was silent for a moment before replying, "Yes," she quietly responded, "I am."

Collecting his thoughts, Daniel was unsure if we wanted to ask the next question that had been on his mind. He knew he cared about her regardless of what she was, but did she care about him? Was it all an act? What would have been his fate had he not found out. Given his situation and their being no light at the end of this tunnel, he decided he would just outright ask. "So, was everything a lie? Was your plan to gather your strength then kill us all?"

"Yes," Hali responded, "But not you, you were different, I would never hurt you."

"How can I believe that? After all I was the one who stabbed you through that night on the ship."

Hali grew silent while Daniel waited for a response. He was convinced she was out for revenge on him. It was his fault after all that she was in this situation. A few moments had past, but still not response. "Well?" Daniel asked.

"That was you?" Hali asked as she tried to remember the events from that night, "You were the one who stuck a sword through me, I remember now, that's how I knew your face." Hali finished as she realized the truth.

"Yes it was me," Daniel said, his voice full of regret, "I am sorry, though, had I known it was you, or you were it, I would have never." Daniel explained, hoping she would forgive him.

"And had I known you and your character, I would have never tried to harm you, but you must understand, it was in my nature. But believe me, I would never harm you, not now that I know you." Hali pleaded, "You are different, you are not cruel like them, you a kind and compassionate."

Before Daniel could respond, a noise from above got louder and louder as someone was making their way down the stairs. Terrified of who it might be, both Hali and Daniel were silent, hoping it was anyone but Charles. As the noise got louder and louder with each step down the squeaky stairs, Daniel tried his best to make out who it was. Daniel was able to make out two figures at the base of the stairs. "August? Felix?" Daniel called out.

"Aye, we have come to take the girl to the captain." Felix answered as he and August approached their cells. "He is going to start tracing and studying that marks on her back."

"Don't you dare touch me!" Hali hissed as Felix entered her cell.

August stood by with a pistol aimed straight at Hali to ensure her cooperation. Felix grabbed a pair of keys and began to unlock her restraints. In a small protest, Hali yanked away from Felix.

"Look, don't make me have to shoot you, you will be seeing the captain, dead or alive." August threatened as he continued to aim his pistol straight for her.

Getting nervous Daniel chimed in, "Hali, please just do what they say. Go along with it for now and I promise you, I will make sure you make it out of this alive.

Being pulled from her cell, Daniel gave Hali a reassuring look. Nodding in agreement, Hali allowed the men to march her up the steps. As they disappeared out of sight, Daniel began formulating a plan. He had to get her out of there and quickly before they reached their destination. Unsure how long it would take his father to translate the map from Hali's markings, he had to think of something. Remembering the bullet still lodged in his leg, he knew it would be tricky. After only fifteen minutes or so, he heard someone heading back down the stairs. Imagining the worst that Hali tried to escape and they cut her through, Daniel was surprised to see it was August.

"August? What are you doing back? Where's Hali?" Daniel asked in a panic.

"She is fine, well she is tied up while the captain is trying to copy the map, but she is alive." August responded as he let himself in to Daniel's cell, carrying a small box.

"What's that?" Daniel asked as his eyes narrowed in on the small box under August's arm.

"Look, just because I have to leave you chained here, doesn't mean I can't pull that slug from your leg." He replied as he started to unload what looked like very old medical equipment from the box. With shaky hands, August began to operate on Daniel's leg. Wincing in pain, Daniel did his best to sit still as the bullet was extracted. Taking a sip of rum, August spit the liquid onto the gaping hole in Daniel's leg.

"Waste not," August said, as he took another sip and repeated the process to sterilize the wound.

"Thank you." Daniel said with sincerity as he watched August sew up the hole in his flesh. "You didn't have to do this."

"Danny boy, I see you as a son, I may be a rotten bastard, but I am a rotten bastard who still cares about you and you not losing that leg to infection." August replied, still slowly stitching the wound. "Your father may not give a damn, but it is what your mother would have wanted."

"You probably remember more of her then I do." Daniel said as he hung his head low.

"Well, unlike your father, she was kind, generous, and beautiful. Boy was she lovely," August began as he started to reminisce, "How she ended up with a pirate, I'll never know. She was always better than us, definitely better than your father, though he was different then."

"How so?" Daniel asked as he watched August finish stitching up his leg.

"Well, your father has always been a rotten and greedy man, but when he was with her, when he was in love, he smiled. Not to mention, a lot less deaths on board." August finished as he let out a small laugh.

"That's how Hali makes me feel," Daniel added. "You have to help her August, I know my father, once he has what he wants, he will surely kill her."

August began to pack up his materials as he started to retreat from the cell. Locking the door back up, August began to head out, ignoring Daniel's pleas for help.

"August!" Daniel called out, "Please."

"I can't." August replied as he headed back up the steps towards the deck.

Sitting in the quiet of the dark, Daniel began to lose hope. He was hoping that August and Felix would be on his side, but he was wrong. There was no one on the ship he could trust and no one who would help him. The light at the end of the tunnel was turning dim as time went on. Trying to rest, Daniel could not help but awaken every few minutes, hoping to see Hali back in the cell across the way, but still nothing. Not knowing if she was alive or dead, Daniel began to grow worried.

As time continued to feel endless, Daniel was able to sleep for a bit. It could have been minutes, hours, days, he was unsure. The exhaustion got the best of him as each short dream he entered took him to see and believe different scenarios outside of his current situation. One dream was that he was a child back in England with his mother, another would transport him to a time when he and his father were first sailing together. A time when Charles wasn't so cruel. Waking up from this obvious dream, Daniel took a look around and even called out for Hali, but yet again, there was no response.

Slipping into one final dream, Daniel had manifested within his mind, a fantasy of Hali and himself together. No pirates, no sea serpents, no Grey Siren and definitely no Captain Charles. This dream was a reality Daniel now hoped for. Just Hali and himself in a small cottage with no worries about them. Just happiness, a feeling Daniel had not felt in a while, a feeling Hali brought back to him like Lazarus returning from the grave. He could feel her flowing silver hair in between his fingers as he held her close while his other hand felt the warmth of her satin skin. Holding her close while the two shared a kiss, only this time there was no pain, no pull back.

Daniel never wanted to leave this world he had manifested, but the sound of a cell door closing brought him back to reality, one where none of these dreams would ever be real. With a quick shake of his head, Daniel woke up as his eyes popped open. If a cell door had closed, maybe that meant Hali had returned. Blinking rapidly to try and see clearly, Daniel softly whispered, "Hali?"

A weak voice came from the cell across from his answered, "Yes."

It was Hali, she was back, and she didn't sound too good. "Hali, are you okay? What did they do to you?" Daniel asked in a panic.

"I'll be fine, just a few bumps and bruises. I've been through worse," Hali replied, trying to sound tough.

"Did my father get what he needed?"

"He was able to draw a rendering of the map from my markings and has set course to follow it," Hali said. "I'm only allowed to live as an insurance policy in case he made a mistake. Or so he has said."

"Do you think he made a mistake in his drawing?"

"No, the map he was able to draw was correct, only a few days journey to get there."

"Then only a few more days he will let you live," Daniel thought out loud. A shiver went through his body as he thought about his last remarks.

Time was not on their side. If a plan was going to be made, it had to be made now. With that, Daniel had an idea. "Hali, what if you healed within these next few days, could you transform back into your serpent form? Then no shackles could hold you back, right?"

"If only it were that easy," Hali said with a small laugh, "Trust me, that thought crossed my mind, but in order to transform into my sea serpent form, I need to be in the *sea*. Those are the rules."

Bringing to light a question Daniel had on his mind, he figured he had nothing to lose in asking what he had been wondering. "So, if you don't mind me asking, how does that whole thing work? I mean you being this legendary creature, and well, a human? Were you born this way?"

"That's a bit of a long story," Hali replied with a small laugh under her breath.

"Well, do you have anywhere to be?" Daniel jokingly replied as he tried to lighten the mood.

"Touché," Hali responded before taking a moment to gather her thoughts. With a deep breath, Hali began to tell her story. "Well, I wasn't always the sea serpent, I was born just an ordinary human girl, a silly one at that. Years ago, so many that even I have lost count, I made a mistake." Sadness filled her voice.

"If you want to stop, it's alright." Daniel said, his voice tender.

"No, its fine, I have just never told anyone this before, and considering I may die in a few days, you may be the first and last." Hali collected herself as she cleared her throat to continue. "Years ago, I met a man, a man I believed to have loved me. His name was Seth. He was a pirate who had made port for a few days, and he promised to take me far away on an adventure to find some legendary treasure. I was silly enough to believe him, to let his promises and his words seduce me."

"Did you love him?" Daniel quietly asked.

"I thought I did, that was until I found out the whole thing was a lie." Hali's tone turned to anger. "He used me and tricked me with his fancy words and vows, but it was an act just to get me into his bed. Eventually, I found out the truth, or rather, the truth found us." Hali paused as she let the memories flood in. Shaking her head, she continued, "One morning, while Seth and I were tangled up in the sheets in his home, we received a visitor. Seth's wife. I had no idea he was married and I was left angry and heartbroken, but not as much as Seth's wife. I tried to apologize, but she would not hear of it. Collecting my things, I left as fast as I could. I locked myself in my home, feeling nothing but heartbreak and guilt. After a few days, I received a knock at my door, and when I opened it, there was Seth's rotting body at my doorstep with his wife standing behind him, an insane look about her face and a sinister smile. I knew I was next to endure the same fate as Seth, and I knew I deserved it." Hali grew quiet.

Breaking the silence Daniel tried to reassure her, "You didn't know he was married, it was not your fault."

"No, it was. He was a pirate. I should have known he was nothing but a rogue. Even after it all, the anger and the heartbreak, seeing his dead body at my feet, I simply went numb. I didn't care what happened to me, whatever she did to me, I had brought it upon myself." Taking in another long breath, Hali continued to reminisce that night as she continued, "Armed with a pistol, she marched me out to a small boat and ordered me to get in it. Sailing into the middle of the ocean, I couldn't help but wonder *why?* Why not just shoot me on land or dump my body in the ocean within the first few minutes of sailing. I knew whatever she had planned for me, it was not going to end well. Once we were an hour from the shore, we stopped the boat. With a pistol still aimed at me, she brought out a piece of parchment and small vile filled with what looked like wine. She ordered me to drink and all I could think was, *Poison, what an easy way to go*. The liquid tasted of toxic chemicals and once I had consumed the entire thing, she recited words in a language I had never heard. Soon I felt like my insides were trying to escape me, bringing me the most excruciating pain I had ever experienced. The woman then threw me overboard and told me something, something I will never forget." Hali paused.

"What did she say?" Daniel asked, intrigued with her story.

"She said, *now you will become the monster you truly are, I am giving you exactly what you wanted. Men will desire you, so much that they will hurt you for your body, they will use you for their own lust and greed, and when they find that you can provide them with nothing and it was all a lie, you will understand your faults and you will understand my pain."*

"You were lied to as well though, she had to understand that, that he deceived you both!" Daniel screamed as he was invested in Hali's story.

"A woman scorned is a dangerous creature," Hali replied as she adjusted herself in her iron cuffs, "After that, she left me in the water to die, just when I thought I was about to meet death, I started to feel a change, a powerful surge taking over my body, I was transforming. That was the night I became the Sea Serpent, and that's when I understood her curse."

"So you have been cursed this whole time?" Daniel asked.

"I see it as a blessing, a second life, one where I was powerful. Even when the men came to hunt me, they were no match for my new strength. She gave me a second life to see the truth behind men's actions. She didn't punish me, she freed me."

This statement left Daniel confused. *How was being turned into a monster considered freedom?* Daniel thought as he absorbed in Hali's story. It was now clear why Hali did not trust pirates, but was she happy in this new life?

Hali continued with her story, trying to answer the questions that must had been burning on Daniel's mind. "It took a few years to understand her words, and only when I was able to figure out how to take on my human form again, did I realize what she meant. I would never age, leaving me always as a target. I discovered the markings on my back and as I ventured town to town, I heard the stories of the Legendary Sea Serpent and the markings upon its back leading to treasure. No doubt poetic justice for the treasure Seth had promised me, as well as his wife. I understood now why men would be coming for me, and you know what? I was ready for them, each greedy and evil man that crossed my path, so I retreated back to where the rumors said I would be and waited."

"So you could have led a normal life and you chose to be the monster and murder men?" Daniel asked in disbelief.

"The minute this curse was placed upon me, a normal life was off the table for me," Hali spat back,

"Why be a human, someone who can easily be betrayed by others when I could be a strong and powerful sea serpent!" Hali exclaimed.

These words began to sink down in Daniel's mind. Maybe she was right, after all, in just the last few days, it was humans who had harmed her so. Living life as a pirate can cause you to really see the worst in people, but Daniel knew it was just a small percentage. Not everyone was the enemy, some were kind. Some humans could be trusted. "What about me?" Daniel inquired as he stared back at Hali through the darkness. "Do you think I am evil too?"

Silence filled the air as Daniel waited for an answer. The only sound in the air was that of the water rocking the ship back and forth as each wave hit the side of the ship. Daniel hung his head low as it was clear Hali was not going to respond. Feeling hurt inside, Daniel came to the conclusion that it must have all been an act. Hali would have turned on him at any moment had she not been too weak. Taking in a deep breath, Daniel let out an audible sigh.

"No," Hali finally replied, "I don't think you are evil, you are different from any man I have ever met."

"Hali, please believe me when I say I would never do anything to hurt you."

Hali sniffled as tears started to cascade down her face, "I know you wouldn't."

"When I promised I would get you out of here, I meant it, I will find a way." Daniel stated with confidence.

Chapter 7

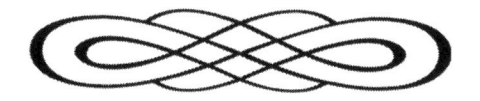

As the sun rose, small beams of light started to shine through the small cracks of the cell walls, causing a bit of light to enter the room. Hali rested as Daniel tried to formulate a plan. He had to get her into the water so she could transform and escape, it was the only way. That was if she was even strong enough to change into her serpent form. Daniel looked across his cell into Hali's, imagining a life where they were together, the life had had recently dreamt of. A life where they could be free and leave all this pirate business behind them. A life where she could learn to trust again. Staring at Hali as she slept, Daniel studied her face. Someone so lovely filled with so much anger and pain that he just wished he could take away. His trance was broken as the sound of footsteps and jangling keys began to fill the room. Hoping for anyone but his father, Daniel waited to see who the visitor was.

"Breakfast," a shaky voice announced.

"Peter?" Daniel asked as an idea started to formulate in his head.

Peter began to approach Daniel's cell with a small plate of food. It was clearly scraps from the crews already eaten breakfast, but it was nice to know his father didn't want them to starve to death. Seeing that Hali was asleep, Peter quietly entered Daniels cell. Getting closer, Daniel spotted the keys he needed.

"Peter you need to help us," Daniel pleaded, "please, just release me from these restraints."

"I was told I can't unshackle you, no matter what. My only job was to make sure you ate, so it looks like I will have to feed you myself." Peter quietly muttered.

"My father is going to kill us unless you help us now!" Daniel said assertively.

"He wouldn't kill his own son, now open up if you want a bite of this biscuit." Peter replied as he raised the piece of stale bread towards Daniel's mouth.

"You don't know him that well, he will take out anyone who stands in his way and sacrifice anyone to get what he wants, you should know that first hand!" Daniel stated, hoping Peter would understand.

Peter's face changed as he let Daniel's words sink in. His eyes filled with guilt as he stared back at Daniel and then again at Hali across the way. "I will be in so much trouble if I do. It will surely be the cat o'nine tails for me, or worse, the plank." Peter mumbled as he thought about it.

"I saved your life, you owe me!" Daniel exclaimed as he looked over Peter's shoulder at the sound asleep Hali. "You can say I overpowered you. Tell him that somehow I escaped from my chains, anything, but please, you are our only hope now."

Looking down at the keys in his hand for a few moments, Peter made his decision, "I'll help you."

Placing the key in the lock of each of Daniel's cuffs, Daniel was finally free. Obtaining the key from Peter, Daniel rushed to Hali's cell and did the same. Hali's unconscious state caused her to fall into Daniel's arms like a rag doll as soon as she was free from her shackles. Lightly tapping his fingers along her pale cheek Daniel tried to wake her. "Hali, Hali wake up."

"Daniel?" Hali groaned as her eyes began to slowly flutter open, "What's going on?"

"I told you I would get us out of here."

"But how?"

"Peter helped us," Daniel replied as he pointed out Peter who was standing just outside her cell. "Now we don't have much time, so we need to move and move fast." Daniel finished as he helped Hali to her feet. "Now, Peter in a few minutes, I need you to come chasing after us on deck."

"What? Why?" Peter asked with a confused expression on his face.

"I have a plan, plus we don't want my father to know you let us out." Daniel stated as he shuffled Hali up the steps towards the deck. "Oh yeah, one more thing," Daniel said as he turned towards Peter before giving him a swift punch to the face.

Peter collected himself after the unexpected hit, "What was that for?"

"To prove we overpowered you, now you should be in the clear. Now wait here so we can get a head start." Daniel instructed as he and Hali ran up the steps.

Once on deck, Daniel and Hali looked around while there eyes adjusted to the light. There was no one in their immediate area. The two carefully headed towards the starboard side of the ship. Almost reaching it, they heard a voice rounding the corner, not just any voice, Captain Charles voice. Daniel grabbed Hali and pulled her behind a few empty barrels that were scattered about. With the plan now needing to move faster, Daniel had to think.

"Daniel, what are we doing?" Hali whispered as she grew concerned.

"I was trying to get you off the ship and into the water," Daniel explained while he peeked his head up, "That way you can transform and get free."

"I don't even know if I am strong enough yet, and besides, what about you? What will your father do to you?" Hali asked with a worried expression on her face.

"Don't worry about me, I'll take a few lashings but I'll be fine."

The two waited for a few moments until the voices grew lighter and lighter as Charles passed by. Once the coast was clear, Daniel and Hali continued more quickly this time around towards the side of the ship. They were moving so fast that they didn't even realize who they were about to run immediately into. Just as they reached the side, there he was, Captain Charles, sword in hand waiting for them.

"I thought I heard a rat behind those barrels, nice try Danny boy, now hand her over." Charles demanded as he aimed the tip of his sword at them both.

Somewhere in the distance, Peter began hollering about their escape as Daniel had instructed. Running out of time and options, Daniel began to lose faith in his plan. He was unarmed with a sword pointed right at him and Hali. Reasoning was his only option.

"You have what you need, you have the map, just let her go." Daniel pleaded as he placed Hali behind him. "I am telling you right now, I will not stop trying to rescue her from you!"

"Why, because you love her?" Charles mocked.

These words floated in the air and into Daniel's ears. His father was right, he did love her. He didn't understand how it could happen so fast, but he knew these feelings were something more. This wasn't just an infatuation. He loved her, all of her. "Yes," Daniel muttered as Hali and Charles both looked at Daniel with shocked expressions lingering on their faces. "Yes I do," Daniel repeated as he turned towards Hali, "I love you Hali."

Facing Daniel, Hali's expression changed from shocked to a small gentle smile as she reached for his hand and intertwined her fingers with his, gleaming Hali quietly said, "I love you too Daniel." As she stood on her tip toes to plant a sweet soft kiss on his lips, almost forgetting their current situation, the moment was interrupted as Charles moved closer, this time bringing the sword under Hali's chin, causing the moment to disappear as they were both snapped back into reality.

"Clearly, this beast has put some sort of spell on you," Charles grumbled as he used his sword to wedge the two apart. "I should slaughter her right here right now so you can snap out of it Daniel!"

By this time, the entire crew had crowded around to watch the show that was taking place. Seeing that Hali was about to say something that may cost her- her life, Daniel quickly chimed in. "Father, please just let her go, and we can put this all behind us. I will stay with you father and become the captain like you have always wanted, I promise. Hali and I will never see each other again," Daniel bargained as he looked at Hali and meant it. He did love her, but he would rather let her go and live then have her be doomed on the ship. Catching Hali's glossed over eyes, he knew she understood his actions.

"So you want me to let her go?" Charles asked. "I let her go, and you will stay with me?"

Reaching his hand out to shake his father's, Daniel confirmed, "Yes, you have my word." Daniel finished as he and Charles shook on it.

"Boys!" Charles called out, "Fetch me some irons!"

"Irons, what for?" Daniel asked, confused. "I thought we had a deal?"

August brought forth a pair of iron shackles as requested. "Now," Charles demanded as he took a step back, his sword still aimed at Hali, "Chain her!"

"What?" Hali and Daniel both exclaimed as August began to cuff her.

"I said I would let her go, and I will, right off that plank." Charles said in a giddy voice as he pointed towards the plank hanging over the side just one deck up. "Try to stop me and I will cleave her to the brisket, right here, right now." As Daniel backed down and with Hali chained, Charles ordered her to march up the steps.

"Father, you can't!" Daniel pleaded before being interrupted by Hali.

"Daniel, it's alright, I accept my fate." Hali calmly said as she threw Daniel a quick wink.

Puzzled at first, Daniel was unsure how she was so calm. Quickly thinking, he realized Hali had a plan. Somehow she will be alright. Following them up the steps as Hali marched towards the plank, it clicked. Once she jumps, she will be free in the sea. Free to transform and escape, a fact that Charles did not know. This would work.

Hali slowly walked down the wooden plank as Charles firmly held out his sword, keeping it positioned at her in case she decided to run back onto the ship. The entire crew gathered around. Some were in shock at what they were about the witness, while others had sinister smiles and looks of joy plastered on their face. Daniel stared intensely, hoping she was right, hoping that this wouldn't end with her at the bottom of the sea.

As Hali reached the end of the plank, Charles asked one last question, "Any last regards wench?"

"You will all pay!" Hali shouted as she confidently leaped off the wooden board and into the sea.

The entire crew, as well as Daniel, bolted towards the side of the ship to see the results. Charles joined as they all scanned the water for a drowning Hali. Their eyes darting back and forth, no one was able to catch sight of her. All they could see was the white foam of the water where she had landed, but no body. After a few minutes, Charles exclaimed, "She must have sunk straight to the bottom!" This was met by cheers from the crew, all except Daniel, who was still anxiously scanning the water. *Maybe she changed and just swam away*, Daniel thought as he tried to comfort his mind.

"I'm sorry Daniel," Peter said as he stood next to Daniel, keeping his eyes fixed on the water as well. "I'm not sure what your plan was, but I'm sure this was not it. All we can hope for is that it was a quick and painless death."

A tear began to roll down Daniel's cheek as he imagined the worst. "She seemed to have her own plan; I just hope she succeeded."

"Alright men, back to work!" Charles commanded. "We need to stay on course if we are to find the treasure!" The crew did what they were told while Charles fixated his attention on the map.

Finally able to rip himself from the ships banister, Daniel walked towards his father, feeling all kinds of emotions, but mostly anger. Breathing hard with both his fists clenched, Daniel approached his father. "What the hell is the matter with you?" Daniel screamed through grinding teeth.

"Is that any way to speak to your Captain? You're lucky I don't chain you back up down below!"

"You are not my Captain! You're barely even my father for that matter!" Daniel started as his voice grew louder and louder, "I loved her! I finally had someone I truly cared about, and you took that away from me!" Daniel continued to shout, causing a scene.

"You're walking a fine line there, Danny boy," Charles replied as he placed his hand on his side, reaching for his pistol. "You can either fall in line, or end up like your little sea wench!"

Feeling his heart racing from the excitement, Daniel didn't want to back down just yet. At this point he would be happy to walk the plank, anything to escape this life. Not sure what to say next, Daniel suddenly had an idea. He knew exactly how to hurt his father the most.

"Fine," Daniel said softly, "but if I am to be sent to my watery grave, this is coming with me!" Daniel yelled as he swiftly grabbed the map of Hali's traced markings from his father's hands. Moving as quickly as possible, he ran to the side of the ship and promptly threw the map in the water. It wasn't more than a second after the piece of parchment had left his hand, that his father charged him, knocking him to the ground. It was too late though; the map belonged to the sea now.

"What have you done?" Charles screamed as he aimed his pistol straight at Daniel's head, as he towered over him.

"Bet you wish you hadn't made the only other copy drown and sink to the bottom of the ocean," Daniel taunted as he didn't even attempt to fight back, accepting his fate and ready to face the consequences of his actions. "Do it," Daniel softly said as the crew began to turn their focus on the situation. "Do it!" he screamed as he looked his father dead in the eyes.

With his pistol still aimed straight for Daniel's head, Charles hesitated as he looked into his son's eyes. "Don't make me do this Danny," Charles calmly said as Daniel continued to stare back intensely. Positioning his finger on the trigger, Charles took a deep breath in.

Time stood still as the crew watched on, not sure what to do, until there was a rumbling from below. Something under the ship caused the Grey Siren to violently rock to the left, causing everyone, including

Charles, to lose their footing. A gun-shot echoed in the air as Charles fell backwards.

"What's going on?" A crew member shouted from below as the ship continued to shake.

"To the cannons!" Charles ordered, leaving Daniel on the floor while he rushed to take control of the helm.

Daniel carefully walked to the side of the ship to catch a glimpse of what was happening below. He knew it had to be Hali in her serpent form, and if she was in her serpent form, then that means the plan worked and she was safe. For now at least. He had hoped she would just swim away and carry on living her life, but it seemed like vengeance was on her agenda. The minute the crew spotted her, they would fire. He had to do something to stop them.

Daniel ran down the steps to stop the men from loading the cannons. He reached Felix and August's station and pleaded with them to stop but was unsuccessful. He only had one other option now, get rid of the cannonballs and gun powder. Daniel began to gather as much as he could and proceeded to throw it overboard.

"What are you doing?" August shouted, "That thing will kill us all!"

"That *thing* is Hali and I am not going to let you hurt her!" Daniel shouted back as he raced back to the top deck with a wooden box of gunpowder.

The ship continued to rock, as cannon blasts filled the air. Trying hard to keep his balance, Daniel continued to look on each side to find where Hali was attacking from. Catching sight of her silhouette swimming below the water, he watched as she leaped from the water and into the ship, puncturing a large hole in the broad side. As more smoke filled the air as the men unsuccessfully attacked Hali, Daniel began to realize the ship was extremely damaged, and it would only be a matter of time before it sank with everyone on it.

The men continued to fire at Charles's command. Realizing that someone had to put an end to this, Daniel raced above towards his father, hoping to seize the fire. Just as he reached his father, ready to try and reason with him, the ship tilted forward as something large weighed down the bow. It was the serpent, it was Hali. She was on the ship, ready to strike.

Hearing the growls, Charles whipped around ready to shoot at Hali, and Hali ready to strike at Charles, but not before Daniel forced himself between the two as he stood in the path of the crossfire. "Enough!" Daniel shouted, bringing a halt to both Hali and Charles.

"Out of the way!" Charles shouted, "I will shoot through you if I have too!"

Hearing this, Hali, still in her serpent form, lunged past Daniel and towards Charles. Pulling the trigger, a stray bullet flew past Hali as she dodged it before knocking Charles to the floor. The impact caused Charles to loose hold of his pistol and was now at the mercy of the sea serpent. Salty droplets of water dripped from Hali's scaly body as she pinned him to the floor. Opening her jaw, causing saliva to add to the already drenched Charles, she was ready to attack.

"Stop!" Daniel shouted, causing Hali to whip her head around. "Hali please, I know he hurt you and you seek vengeance on him, but please for my sake don't do this." Daniel explained as he looked down at his father's cowardly expression. "I love you Hali, truly I do, but he is still my father."

Now the entire crew was watching, frozen in place by fear to even try to fight. Hali's mouth slowly closed. Her hardened expression began to grow soft as she and Daniel continued to keep focus on one another. Daniel had not seen her this close and clearly in this form, not since the day he stabbed her through with his sword under the cover of night. Now seeing her in a new light, he knew she was not a monster. She could choose to let his father live. He knew if he didn't put a stop to this, he wouldn't be sure if he could forgive her. "Please Hali, just let him go," Daniel begged as he placed a hand on her cold silver scaled skin. "We can leave, just the two of us, together."

Hali gazed back at Daniel and began to back away. A still terrified and unarmed Charles stayed frozen in place as he watched as his life was spared. "I owe you my life," Charles said in a shaky voice, "I'm sorry Daniel, for everything."

"This will be the last time you ever see me," Daniel said as he crouched down towards his father, "I am starting a new life. I hope you can now see what this life, the life you chose, has cost you. Now if I were you, I'd get yourself and the crew off this ship before it sinks." Daniel finished, his voice filled with relief and disdain.

"Danny boy," Charles started as his face turned from fear to sadness.

"Goodbye father." Daniel finished as he walked towards Hali, climbing on her back before the two of them plunged into the water.

The whole crew raced to the side of the ship in disbelief of what just unfolded before their eyes. Seeing Daniel riding the sea serpent in the water below, their eyes followed them until they had fully disappeared. The crew was unsure what to do as the ship continued to sink and fall apart.

"Captain?" Felix called up as he watched Charles finally stand to his feet, "What do we do now?"

Looking out at his broken ship and his confused crew, and finally at the water he watched his son disappear into, Charles gave his last command. "Abandon ship."

Epilogue

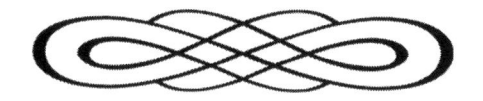

The sun had finally started peeking through the grey clouds that had begun to depart. A rainy night brought the smell of fresh moss in the morning as the sun began to soak up the puddles that lingered in the grass. The green from the plant life glowed in Wicklow Ireland, every morning was fresh and new.

As the sun continued to rise, a ray of light shined through the windows of the little white cottage on the top of the emerald hill. The thatched roof had done its job in keeping everything inside nice and dry. Nothing but a pleasant awakening for the couple inside.

Still tucked under the thick quilt, Daniel and Hali released their embrace to each let out a much needed stretch. "Good morning my love," Daniel whispered as he parted his brides silver hair to plant a soft kiss on her forehead

"Good morning Daniel," Hali mumbled as she rolled in the bed, still trying to wake up.

It had been three magical years since Daniel said goodbye to his father and to the life of piracy. Choosing Hali was something he would never regret. Just as quickly as their love blossomed, so did the next chapter in their lives. After leaving the Grey Siren, Daniel and Hali had not heard from, nor heard of for that matter, of Captain Charles the Dread. It had seemed that he had completely retired from his life of piracy, leaving Daniel and Hali to live a happy and peaceful life.

Daniel worked hard to make the dreams he had while imprisoned on the Siren come true. The one where he and Hali had lived happily ever after in a small home of their own was the dream he could not let go of, and the dream he made a reality after the two departed from the ship that day years ago. "I have to get ready to go," Daniel said as he let out a big yawn while bringing himself to his feet.

"No, just a little longer, the fish will still be there, just come back to bed for a bit longer, please," Hali pleaded as she lifted the quilt, inviting Daniel back into bed.

Daniel let out a small huff accompanied with a small smile, "Fine, but just five more minutes," Daniel finished as he crawled back under the covers while Hali wrapped her arms around him.

Every morning was the same. Daniel would get up to start preparing himself for work and Hali would always convince him to stay a little longer. Taking a job as a fisherman in the town, meant early mornings if he was going to make the coin he needed. Hali was all the riches Daniel needed, so he always gave in to her cunning ways.

"Those few fish I don't catch are now coming straight out of that new dress fund," Daniel teased as he softly kissed Hali's neck.

"I look better in your shirts anyways," Hali giggled as she rolled on top of Daniel, pinning his arms down, "Now you're stuck with me forever."

"Not a bad place to be stuck forever if you ask me," he replied as he pulled Hali's face to meet his.

Daniels lips met Hali's as the two became lost in their own passions, unable to pry each other away. It was clear Hali had finally found a new purpose in life, love. No longer did she need to keep her serpent form to feel safe and powerful. Daniel did both of these for her now. Wrapping his arms around Hali as the two continued to remain interlocked under the warmth of the quilt, all of their fears and doubts from their past lives simply faded away. They were rewriting their own stories, their own new fates.

Daniel strategically placed his lips on Hali's shoulder, her weak spot. It worked just as Daniel had planned as Hali reacted to his warm breath on her skin and let go of Daniel's arms as she moaned in response.

Rolling on to Hali, Daniel was now in charge, "Works every time," Daniel laughed before giving Hali one last kiss.

"I fall for it every morning," Hali grumbled.

"You can try again tomorrow," Daniel said as he began to dress into his works clothes.

"Maybe I like to fall for it, maybe I am just playing dumb," Hali said flirtatiously as she gathered her hair to one side, covering her shoulder.

"Well I am glad you do," Daniel winked as he slipped his feet into his boots, ready to work.

"Let me walk you to the door," Hali said as she got out of bed, draping the quilt over her body as a dress.

Daniel gathered the last few items he needed to have a successful day at work. Stuffing a roll into his mouth, Daniel made his way to the door. "I love you, I'll see you at sundown." Daniel said as he gave Hali a kiss on the cheek.

"I love you, be safe."

Daniel exited the cottage and began making his way down the hill towards the town. As Daniel almost reached the bottom, just before the cottage would be out of view, Daniel looked back. Squinting, he could see Hali still in the door frame, watching Daniel until he was out of view, just like she did every morning.

With a smile he was certain Hali probably couldn't see, Daniel waved as he continued out of view. The little things like this that caused Daniel to have a permanent smile and endless happiness in his life since the day that he first laid eyes on Hali. Since that day he made the decision to change his path in life and follow another. He had never looked back at his old life. It was a distant memory. Though his father would mingle in his thoughts from time to time, his overwhelming feelings and love for Hali and the life they had built together seemed to ground him in the present. A life that he thought could only exist in a dream. A dream that he made a reality. A reality full of the one thing he always wanted. Love. And love was what he had. These thoughts always loomed in his mind as he walked to town each morning, completely enveloped in peace and happiness.

Printed in Great Britain
by Amazon